MYSTERY GUEST

ALSO BY MAREN STOFFELS

ESCAPE ROOM

FRIGHT NIGHT

ROOM SERVICE

STRANGER DANGER

NO ESCAPE

DEEP WATER

MYSTERY GUEST

MAREN STOFFELS

Translated by Laura Watkinson

DELACORTE PRESS

Delacorte Press
An imprint of Random House Children's Books
A division of Penguin Random House LLC
1745 Broadway, New York, NY 10019
penguinrandomhouse.com
rhcbooks.com

Originally published in paperback and in Dutch by Uitgeverij Leopold,
a division of WPG Kindermedia BV, Amsterdam, in 2024.

Editor: Alison Romig
Cover Designer: Casey Moses
Interior Designer: Michelle Gengaro-Kokmen
Production Editor: Jamie Johnson
Managing Editor: Tamar Schwartz
Production Manager: Liz Sutton

Library of Congress Cataloging-in-Publication Data is available upon request.
ISBN 979-8-217-12216-5 (trade) — ISBN 979-8-217-12217-2 (ebook)

The text of this book is set in 11.25-point Warnock Pro.

Manufactured in the United States of America
1st Printing

The authorized representative in the EU for product safety and compliance
is Penguin Random House Ireland, Morrison Chambers, 32 Nassau Street,
Dublin D02 YH68, Ireland, https://eu-contact.penguin.ie.

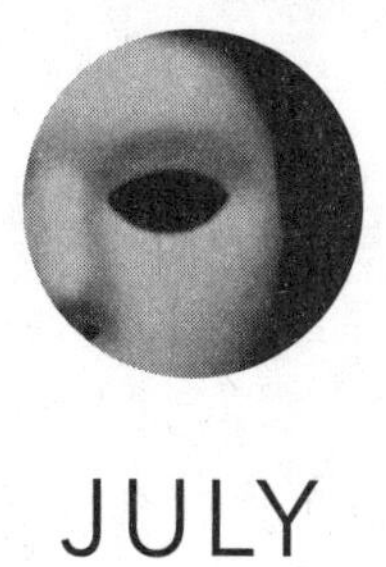

JULY

SUMMER VACATION

PIP

What have I done?
Maria and I . . .
She has to come back.
I need to tell her I love her.
Tell me it isn't true . . .
Tell me I didn't kill her.

CODY

Maria let me into her life right away.
I think she was hoping for someone like me to come along.
She really shouldn't have let me in.
I was the one who killed her.

NORAH

I hated Maria.
Yeah, sorry, but that's just how it was.
I don't have a better word for it.
She had to die.

MARIA & PIP

Please just open it.

I throw a second stone at Pip's window; the sound echoes along the silent street.

Any minute now, her mom and dad are going to wake up.

Pip's phone must be off. My messages aren't reaching her, which is why I walked over here.

I throw a third stone, a bigger one this time.

Is she really sleeping that deeply? Or is she deliberately ignoring me?

The idea of being ignored by Pip chills me. Where am I going to go if she doesn't let me in?

Maybe she's still mad about the fight this afternoon, and that's why she's leaving me outside in the middle of the night.

But then finally her curtains open, and I feel my heart leap.

I did it.

Pip slides her window open, leans on her windowsill, and looks at me. She doesn't even seem surprised to see me here at this time of night.

She nods at the neighbors' roof, which runs underneath her window.

Does she seriously expect me to climb up there?

I look at the drainpipe. It has a few ridges sticking out on the sides. I've seen people climb them in movies. It always looks so easy.

I grab the drainpipe and plant my sneakers on the first ridge.

The first time, I slip back down. The second time, I scrape my bare arm on the brick wall. But the third time is the charm.

From the roof it's easy to get through Pip's window. She pulls me over the windowsill, my legs sliding in last and flopping onto the floor like I'm a rag doll.

It's not the coolest of entrances, but I can't help laughing.

It must be the sense of relief because I managed the climb. Or maybe just because Pip's here.

Even though she's *always* here, I'm afraid that one day she won't be.

Jax bumps his head against my cheek. Pip's ginger tomcat is always happy to see me.

I sit up and scratch Jax behind his ears.

"What do you want?" Her tone is abrupt, so she clearly hasn't forgotten our fight. "It's the middle of the night."

"I know . . . I . . ." I don't get any further than that before the tears start.

"Maria . . ." Pip sits down on the floor beside me and wraps her arms tightly around me.

I breathe in her scent. She smells like the vanilla perfume I gave her for her birthday.

"It's Ferris," I begin. Of course it's Ferris. Whenever I cry, it's always because of my brother.

When he went away, I hoped that things at home would stop revolving around him, but strangely it's even worse than before.

Mom is always crying, and Dad's gotten even quieter than usual.

After visiting hours, I know I have to steer well clear of both of them unless I want to get yelled at.

Everything still revolves around my brother.

"He's coming home tomorrow. On probationary release."

As I say the words, my stomach flips again. Pip knows what this means.

She's the only one I've told about Ferris.

Part of the story, I mean, because I never tell anyone everything.

"How long is he staying?"

"All summer." Again, it dawns on me what that means. "All summer" is six weeks. Six very long weeks.

"Can they just do that?" Pip looks kind of pale.

"Apparently they can." When my mom and dad told me, I thought I was losing my mind. How could Ferris suddenly be coming home for six weeks? They'd paid a fortune to get him into that center. He could have spent the summer there, couldn't he?

"And now?"

6

"And now the summer is going to be a disaster."

"We are not going to let that happen," says Pip. The word "we" makes me feel a bit better.

"How about we do something fun tomorrow?" she suggests.

"What kind of fun?" I look back over my shoulder. It's pitch-dark outside, but I know what's out there. Rows of houses, the woods, the fields, cows, and then the highway.

"There's nothing fun around here."

"There's me."

I look at Pip. I wish that were enough, but it's not.

When Ferris is home, I'm going to need three Pips to get me through those weeks. And probably even that wouldn't be enough.

Pip sits down on her bed. Jax immediately snuggles up on her lap. "How about we go swimming at our lake tomorrow?"

I sit down beside her. "*Our* lake?"

"That's what it is, isn't it?" Pip looks at me. Her green eyes never look directly at mine but always dance around them a little, as if looking at me is too much of a challenge.

There's something cute about it.

"Sure is." I run my finger down her cheek. "You still mad about this afternoon?"

"A bit." Pip turns her face away. "You called me 'safe.'"

I already suspected that was what was bothering her. When I'd said that, Pip winced and said she had to go home.

Pip probably thinks I don't notice when she clams up, but I can see the signals from miles away.

It's like I got an instruction manual for Pip when we got to know each other.

It's not a thick manual. I finished it in no time.

I know exactly what I can and can't do with her. I know her inside out.

"So?" I say defensively.

"'Safe' is the same as 'boring.'"

"That's simply not true." I would *never* call her boring again. The last time I did that, she ignored me for two days. They were the longest two days of my life. "'Safe' and 'boring' are definitely not the same thing."

I think of all the times Pip was there for me this year. Ferris's court case, all that trouble with Mike . . .

Mike.

No, don't think about him.

But he still lingers, like a nasty aftertaste in my mouth. I'm scared he's going to suddenly return to our town one day.

What would it feel like to see him again?

"Can I make it up to you?" I say, changing tactics. I lean forward, but Pip shakes her head.

"Not like that."

"You sure?"

"Sure."

"Then what do I have to do?" I look at her top lip, which is covered in freckles. In the summer, she always gets a freckle mustache from the sun. She really hates it.

I don't. I think it's cute.

Like everything about Pip. Even her name is sweet.

8

"What do you want? Do I have to tell you how attractive you are? How sexy? How—"

"Maria . . ." Pip shakes her head, but I can see in her eyes that she's almost over it.

"How wildly desirable, how fun, how fabulous, how—"

Before I can continue, Pip shuts me up with a kiss.

She puts her arms around me again, and I feel . . . *safe*.

"What's going on?" Pip's dad is suddenly standing in the doorway. Startled, I let go of his daughter. Why didn't we hear him coming?

"Sir, I . . ."

"It's the middle of the night!" Pip's dad growls. "How did you even get in here?"

I glance at the window.

"You need to go home, young lady."

As I walk toward the window, he shakes his head.

"Please use the front door."

That guy really hates me.

At first, I thought it was because he didn't want his daughter dating a girl, until Pip told me about her ex. Seems he did like her . . .

"Yes, of course. Sir." I look at Pip, who seems to be struggling not to laugh.

She's never been bothered by the fact that her dad doesn't like me. And that's always given me a certain peace of mind.

No matter what anyone does or says, Pip will always be on my side.

Always.

I said she was safe, didn't I?

"See you tomorrow," says Pip as I leave her room.

"We'll see about that," I hear her dad reply.

Outside, it's still pitch-dark, but strangely I feel a lot lighter.

Pip recharged my batteries. She even made me forget about my brother for a little while.

As I'm walking home, my phone buzzes.

Is it Pip? To say she misses me already?

But no, it's an unknown number. With a weird profile picture: a greenish mask with just one visible eye.

MYSTERY GUEST, it says.

My scalp tingles. I stop beneath one of the lampposts.

And how did this person get my number?

Then I see the message. It's short but powerful.

MYSTERY GUEST:

Bored?

MARIA & MYSTERY GUEST

click on the profile picture, but that one eye is totally un-recognizable.

Who could it be?

I look at the message on my screen again, but there are no clues.

Why would a stranger ask me if I'm bored?

I look around. The street is silent, as it always is at this late hour. And at all the other times of the day, to be honest.

Our town gives the word "boring" a whole new meaning.

I click on the number. The phone rings out three times before the line goes dead.

No voicemail, nothing.

Who *is* this?

For a moment, Norah flashes through my mind. Could the eye behind the mask belong to Pip's ex?

Maybe. I don't even know what color Norah's eyes are. I try to avoid her as much as possible.

Unfortunately, though, she keeps turning up, just when

I'm not expecting her. In a town like this, you can't avoid each other forever.

Or maybe it's Mike?

I feel anxious at the thought that he got a new phone so he could send me messages.

No, Mike wouldn't do that.

The guy knows he needs to stay as far away as possible from the town and from me.

Doesn't he?

My thumbs hover over the keyboard.

What should I reply?

Bored?

Whoever it is, they've hit the nail on the head.

MARIA:

Always.

I wait a few seconds. My message has been sent.

My heart is pounding against my rib cage, but if I'm honest, it's not an unpleasant feeling.

It's a bit like when I used to take money from my mom's or dad's wallets. Not for the money but for the feeling it gave me.

They sometimes used to notice that something was missing, but they didn't know why. Carrying a secret around with you, knowing something that only *you* know—it makes you feel alive.

Really alive.

And now I'm talking to someone called Mystery Guest.

I look at the profile picture again. If Norah is behind the mask, I'm going to go crazy.

That girl has been out to destroy me right from the start, and sometimes I'm afraid she'll succeed.

She just kept stirring up trouble between me and Pip. I'm still scared that she'll manage to get Pip to leave me.

What am I supposed to do if Pip's not in my life anymore?

The past few weeks, Norah seems to have been keeping a low profile, but I know it's just a matter of time, because she always resurfaces eventually.

She hates me.

Her instruction manual is way shorter than Pip's. It only has one line: *Stay as far away from her as possible.*

My phone buzzes again, making my heart rate rocket.

MYSTERY GUEST:

Let's play a game.

MARIA & HER MOM AND DAD

"Maria? Did you hear what I said?"

The next morning, my eyes are glued to the screen of my phone as I chew my second piece of toast without tasting it.

Why did Mystery Guest promise me a game, and then I didn't hear from them again?

Maybe it was just someone at school playing a lame joke. I can think of a few guys in my class who are dumb enough to do something like this.

But I still go on staring at my phone. Because what if this is real?

Then a new message arrives. But it's from Pip.

PIP:

Our date is still on.

I'll leave Dad at home.

I smile.

"Maria?" my mom says.

"What?" Sighing, I put down my phone.

"Would you stop by the baker's later to get some cake?"

"Cake?" I look at her. "What's the celebration?"

"You know, Ferris is coming home this afternoon?"

"That's no reason for cake."

"Maria." My dad's voice is tense. It has been all morning. Mom's looking forward to Ferris coming home, but I'm not so sure about Dad.

My dad and Ferris never got along that well. He was always my mom's favorite.

But Mom is Dad's favorite, so he always stands up for Ferris whenever I say anything negative about him.

"Okay," I say. "I'll go get some cake after I go swimming."

MARIA & PIP

Pip is sitting on her towel when I get to the lake. There's no one else around. It's always quiet here.

There are no restaurants, no spectacular slides. Most kids go to the bigger lake in the next town.

It probably doesn't help that this lake has a view of an old warehouse that has been abandoned for years. There's something sinister about the place. But the lake is nice and quiet, which makes it the perfect place to be together without being disturbed.

"Hey, you're here." Pip perks up.

"Of course I'm here."

I lay my towel next to hers. The first time we came here, there was an arm's length between our towels. Now it's just a few grains of sand.

"You been swimming already?" I ask.

"No way. It's much too cold."

"Really?" When I put my foot in the water, it stings. "Cold" is an understatement. It's like an ice bath.

When I walk deeper in, it's like my skin is being attacked by thousands of needles.

"You're not *actually* going to swim, are you?" Pip shouts from her towel.

I take a deep breath. "That is exactly what I'm going to do."

"You really are crazy!"

"I know."

And then I start running. With big leaps, I head deeper into the lake until I can't reach the bottom any longer, and I fall forward. When I'm underwater, it's like my heart stops.

But as I surface, it's beating more strongly than ever.

The sun warms my cold body while Pip chats away. She's talking about her summer job at the animal shelter.

"It's a good thing I rescued that golden retriever," I say, "or you wouldn't have gotten the job."

Pip smiles. "You're right. I only found out about the shelter because of you. And it's the best job ever."

It really does seem to be the perfect job for her: helping poor little animals that no one wants anymore.

"A new labrador came in yesterday," says Pip. "A brown one. I'd love to take him home with me."

"Then why don't you?"

"My mom and dad. They think one cat in the house is enough."

"Who gives a damn about your mom and dad? He'd be your dog, wouldn't he?"

Pip smiles and plants a kiss on my cheek. "I'm not like you."

"Maybe you should be a bit more like me. And give less of a damn."

Pip rolls onto her back and looks up at the sky. I know she's thinking about what I said.

Pip could do with being a bit tougher. And maybe I could be a bit less tough.

That's what happens naturally when we're together—at least, that's how it feels. Pip would never have let anyone into her room in the middle of the night before, and I could never have stayed with anyone for more than a day. Just because I'm so easily bored.

Pip and I watch the clouds drifting by. There was a lot of rain last night after I got back from Pip's, but luckily it's going to stay dry today.

I sit up and check my phone yet again.

"Who's that?" Pip also sits up beside me. "What's that mask?"

There's no going back. She's already seen it.

"Someone who's sending me messages," I say. "I got the first one when I left your place last night."

"But who is it?" Pip pulls my phone from my hands and reads the brief conversation. "'Mystery Guest'? Why did you reply? It's probably some kind of hacker. Before you know it, all of your personal details will be out there in public!"

I snatch my phone back. "It's not a hacker."

"You'd better just block the number."

I shake my head. "I want to find out what kind of game MG wants to play."

"You're abbreviating their name already?" Pip raises her eyebrows. "And what if the game is something dangerous?"

"So much the better."

"Maria . . ."

Pip doesn't get it. She's happy living in a neighborhood where everyone has the same front door, living a life where every Friday evening is pizza night and she watches cheesy rom-coms with her mom and dad. She doesn't care that Outcast is the only club for miles around and that the same people go there every week.

She is totally fine with her life being exactly as it is.

"Are you really *always* bored?" Pip says, giving me a sidelong glance.

"Not *always*." I claw up a handful of sand through my towel and give it a squeeze. "Ninety percent of the time."

There's silence for a moment.

"And the other ten percent?"

I smile. "Then I'm in trouble."

At that moment, a message arrives. My heart skips a beat, but then I see that it's from my mom.

MOM:

Get something with strawberries. They're your brother's favorite.

I swipe the message away. I don't like strawberries, but that doesn't seem to matter.

With a deep sigh, I fall back onto my towel.

"What's wrong?"

"My mom wants me to get cake. Because Ferris is coming home today."

"Want me to come with you?"

"To buy cake?"

"Yeah. And to your place too?"

Pip has brought this up so many times already. I shade my eyes with my hands so that I can look at her.

"Why would you want to?"

"I'd like to meet your mom and dad. And I only know your brother from a distance."

"Count yourself lucky."

"I'd still like to come with you."

"Another time," I say, blowing Pip off. Maybe it makes complete sense that she wants to get to know my life, particularly because we've been together for months, but I still don't want that to happen.

Pip is a different part of my life. A better part.

I don't want to mix that up with the bad part.

You don't stir pickle juice into your chocolate milk, do you?

Then another message comes in.

"Your mom again?"

But this time, the mask is on my screen. Finally! A reply!

MYSTERY GUEST:

Come to this address at 12.

I see a map with a red pin in it. Did they seriously just send me a location?

Where is it?

Even when I zoom in, I don't recognize the place. Looks like it's somewhere in the middle of the woods.

"Maria? Is it that creep again? What did they send you?"

I turn my phone away from Pip. "Nothing."

"Wasn't that a map I saw? You're not going anywhere, are you?"

"No."

"Maria . . ."

Pip knows me. Not 100 percent, but better than anyone else does.

"What?" I try to keep my expression neutral.

"You do not want to do that," Pip insists. "You have no idea who they are or what they want, and they're probably some kind of pervert like Mike, and . . ."

Mike.

I don't want to think about him, but Pip mentioning his name sends it all flashing through my head like a movie. That night at Outcast, the moments on the highway, and then in the back seat of his convertible . . . "Mystery Guest isn't a pervert like Mike" is all I say. "It's just someone who's bored, like me."

"You don't know that."

"Neither do you." I shove my phone into my backpack.

"You know what happened to Shannon."

"Are you seriously going to bring up Shannon?" I look at Pip. "This is something completely different."

"I mean it," says Pip. "You are *not* going to that location."

MARIA & MIKE

To my right is just bushes, but the directions say I need to leave the road here.

That can't be right, can it?

I look again, but the pin really is to my right.

So I have to go into the bushes here.

A car slows down behind me. When I turn to look, I see the red paint. Even before I can see who's driving, I freeze.

Red paint . . .

That red paint . . .

It can only be one person.

"Maria!" Mike, resting his arm on the car door, is looking at me. "What are *you* doing here?"

It's a few seconds before I can even breathe.

Did he seriously ask me what I'm doing here?

What's *he* doing here?!

He left town and moved miles and miles away.

No distance will ever feel like enough, but the thought that he wasn't walking around our little town anymore made me breathe more easily.

When he left, it felt like I'd won.

And now he's here?

"I'm back," says Mike, as if he can read my mind. "Just for the summer. Helping my dad with his business."

I'm still standing there in front of his car, stunned.

"Did you know he opened a campsite?"

Of course I did. I ride my bike past his dad's farm nearly every day.

And every time I do, I'm relieved when I don't see Mike's red convertible in the driveway.

I avoid Mike's dad too. Whenever he shows his face in town, I steer well clear.

"So you'll be seeing me around for the next few weeks." Mike looks at me. "That'll be nice, right?"

He doesn't wait for my reply, just steps on the gas.

I look at the license plate. I still know it by heart.

MM-FE-1.

He said it meant "Mike & Maria—For Ever—1."

That's what he said that night at Outcast, anyway. After that, everything changed.

Why is he back? He knows what everyone in town thinks about him now, doesn't he?

And why now?

I think about Mystery Guest. The thought of following instructions from Mike makes me want to throw up.

Mike.

He's back.

So now I won't have just Ferris around all summer, but Mike too.

This minefield is getting way too crowded.

I watch the car disappear from view.

I had no idea how it would feel to see him again after so long, but it's even worse than I feared.

It was so casual, the way he just talked to me. It's not right. It's almost like he's not scared of the consequences of coming back here. What have I missed? Since when has *he* been in charge?

A shiver runs right through my body.

"Mike . . ." I whisper. "What are you doing here?"

MARIA & MYSTERY GUEST

When my heart has finally stopped pounding quite so hard, I step into the bushes. Whether Mystery Guest is Mike or not, I need to know what kind of game is waiting for me.

The undergrowth is pretty dense, so it takes me a while to find a way in. But then I spot an opening.

MG has been here before me. I can see faint footprints in the soil.

And they've broken off a few branches to make a way through.

What if it *is* Mike?

Is that why he drove past just now? To check if I'd accepted his invitation?

Seems like quite a coincidence that he'd be driving past just as I get here, right?

In my head, I hear the echo of Pip's voice making me promise not to come here. She even mentioned Shannon . . .

Shannon was in school with us. I barely knew her.

Until after she died.

Suddenly she became like a close friend, because Pip and I know *everything* about her now.

We scoured all her social media, looking for information.

I know her friends, her hobbies, her ex-boyfriend, who the immediate suspect was.

Pip and I even went to her funeral. We kept our distance, of course, because we hadn't received an invitation.

But we wanted to experience every second of it, to see if we could discover something. A clue, something the police had overlooked.

But her murder is still unsolved. Shannon's death remains a mystery.

And I can't stand that. I *need* to know how things fit together.

Phone in hand, I walk forward. The directions say I have just a short way to go.

I come to a clearing, surrounded by trees.

At the center of the clearing, there's a small table with three green glass bottles on it. And a red-and-white checkered table-cloth, as if this is some kind of cozy little picnic.

I glance around, but there's no sign of movement.

Whoever MG is, they've already left.

I look back at the table. The idea that Mike is behind this suddenly seems ridiculous.

Mike wouldn't go to so much trouble, not for anything. Coming here for the summer to "help" his dad is probably just going to involve sleeping late and letting his old man cook for him.

I take in the three bottles. Now I notice that their screw caps are different colors: white, yellow, and green.

There's an envelope on the table with my name written on it in sweeping handwriting that I don't recognize.

I take another look around just to make sure, but there's still no sign of anyone.

What is all this?

I pick up the envelope and open it. The rustling of the paper sounds so loud in this quiet place.

Inside the envelope is a small rectangular card with the same elegant lettering on it.

My eyes rush along the lines.

Welcome to the first game.
In front of you are three bottles,
each with a different liquid inside.
Choose one of the bottles, film yourself
drinking the contents, and send me the video.
And then I'll give you another challenge.

I'm supposed to drink one of them?

And film myself doing it?

I glance at the bottles. All three look exactly the same, except for the different caps.

What's inside them?

I quickly read the last few lines on the card.

White you'll like, but it won't challenge you.
Yellow will challenge you, but it won't break you.
Green will break you, but it won't kill you.

I look at the green cap. Whatever's inside that bottle is clearly the biggest risk. But what is it?

I put down the card and pick up the bottle. Cautiously I unscrew the green cap, as if it might explode at any moment.

I raise the bottle to my nose and sniff. I can't smell anything. It could just be water.

Should I try a drop?

I hear Pip's voice in my ear again: *You do not want to do that.*

Maybe she's right. I have no idea what's in there. It could poison me.

I turn to leave, but then I pause.

Isn't this exactly what I wanted?

Something to defeat the constant boredom?

Plus, I'm never going to find out who's behind the mask if I walk away now. Then my boring life will go on just as it did before.

The only excitement in my life right now is because of Ferris and Mike. And Norah, who's sure to turn up again soon.

And that's not a good sort of excitement. It just makes my stomach churn.

Whoever this Mystery Guest is, they're making sure that this summer is not a complete disaster.

You really are crazy, Pip yelled at me when I jumped into the ice-cold lake. And she was right.

I don't want to live with my foot on the brake like she does. I want to go full throttle.

"Okay," I say. "Here goes."

Without stopping to think about it, I pick up the middle bottle, the one with the yellow cap, and I open it. I point my camera at myself, and I hit record.

Without sniffing the contents, I bring the bottle to my lips and take a swig.

Yellow will challenge you, but it won't break you.

Nothing happens at first. I down the liquid in a few gulps and let out a loud burp.

But then it's like a thousand needles are sticking into my throat. I drop the bottle and fall to my knees.

What is it?

I reach into my bag for a bottle of water, but I don't have one.

It's like my body's on fire. I need water. Now!

My eyes are streaming. My vision blurs.

"Help!" I claw at my throat, but it doesn't do any good. The liquid's burning my throat and my insides.

Tears pour down my cheeks. My back's sweating. My head's burning. It's like my body's about to explode.

"What did you . . ." I splutter. "What did you give me?"

I need water, or I'm going to lose my mind.

Then I look at the bottle with the white cap.

White you'll like, but it won't challenge you.

I snatch it from the table and try to twist off the cap. I can't unscrew it at first because my hands are shaking so much, but then finally the cap comes off. Without hesitating, I raise it to my lips.

It can't get any worse than this, can it?

I recognize the flavor with the first gulp: It's milk.

I drink it greedily until the entire bottle's empty.

As the burning pain eases, my eyes stop watering. I point the camera at myself again and look into the lens.

"Happy?" I yell, and then I send the video.

Collapsing, I look at the bottle on the ground next to me. The yellow cap is lying beside it among the pine needles.

What the hell was inside that bottle?

Must have been some kind of chili pepper, which was why I felt like I was burning up. And I know milk can help with that. I watched a video about it online once.

Yellow will challenge you, but it won't break you.

Then I start laughing. I can't help it. I'm laughing as if I've never seen anything so funny before.

I'm sitting here, in the middle of the woods, with three bottles in front of me.

Am I going crazy?

Sure am!

But it also feels like a victory. MG probably thought I'd be too chicken, but I went ahead and drank it anyway.

Whatever was in that bottle, it didn't break me. Just like the description promised.

Nothing scary happened, not like Pip thought it would. Whoever MG is, they don't want to kill me, or it would have already happened by now.

I look at the green bottle, which is still on the table. The description said whatever's in that bottle would break me. What if I'd actually drank it? What kind of state would I be in now?

Then my phone buzzes.

No compliments about how brave I was—nothing. Just a simple question: Want to keep going?

I lower my phone.

It's really dumb of me to even consider it.

Why would I let myself be tortured again?

But on the other hand . . . I did choose it myself. I could have gone for the white bottle, the one with ordinary milk in it.

But I didn't do that.

Because I wanted to find out how bad it would be.

In fact, I was tempted to go for the bottle with the green cap!

I stare at the profile pic with the mask. I've never seen it before, and that eye could be anyone's. It could be Mike's, Norah's, Ferris's, even Pip's . . .

I think about Pip, with those big, innocent eyes of hers.

The same shade of green as in the picture.

I burst out laughing.

Pip.

My Pip? Mystery Guest?

What kind of weird philosophical answer is that?

I'm about to type something back, but they beat me to it.

I hesitate. Five games—that suddenly sounds like an infinite number.

32

I look at their promise, written there in black and white.

Will they keep their word? I stare at the profile pic again, as if I might be able to see through the mask.

My thoughts return to Shannon. When she was found dead, the police questioned everyone in town. A detective even interrogated Pip and me, but they soon realized we didn't have any useful information.

Her murderer is still out there. It could be anyone.

With Mystery Guest, it's the same. It could be *anyone*.

And I won't find out who it is unless I complete the five games, whatever they might be.

MARIA & CODY

"That one, please." Reluctantly I point at the strawberry shortcake. I'd rather have gone for the apple pie beside it, but my mom just sent me a reminder that the dessert has to be something with strawberries.

I run my tongue over my sore lips, which are still tingling from the burning liquid.

What was it? What if it makes me really sick?

But I don't think it will. Then it would already have happened, wouldn't it?

I watch the baker pack up the cake and place it on the counter.

"That'll be thirteen ninety-five."

I hand her the twenty that my mom gave me this morning. "Thanks."

What was inside the bottle with the green cap? Maybe I should have taken it with me, and then I could have tried it at home . . .

You really are crazy.

"There you go." The woman gives me my change, and then, suddenly serious, she looks at me. "By the way, did you know . . ."

Halfway through her sentence, she falls silent and shakes her head.

"Never mind." She waves it aside. "None of my business."

"What is it?"

"Well . . ." She pauses. "Apparently Mike Swan is back."

When I hear his name, it's like an electric shock.

My blood rushes to my head as I reply, "I know. I already ran into him."

"I don't get what he's doing here. He knows what we think of him, doesn't he?"

I grab the cake box off the counter. "Yeah . . ."

"Everyone's on your side, sweetheart," the baker says as I close the door behind me. "Don't you forget that."

On my way home, I see people looking at me. They have the same look of pity on their faces as the baker did.

Mike Swan—from now on, the only topic of conversation is going to be him. And me.

Because if you mention his name, you automatically mention mine. We're inextricably linked, whether I like it or not.

It's warm outside, but there are big clouds in the sky. They said it was going to stay dry today, but I don't believe it.

"Sorry, can I ask you something?" says a voice behind me. Someone else who wants to talk about Mike?

This summer really is going to be a complete disaster.

But when I turn around, I'm looking into the face of a boy with a green baseball cap and deep brown eyes.

I've never seen him before. He's not from our town. I'm sure I'd have remembered a guy like him.

He's handsome.

No, he's breathtaking.

"What . . ." I fall silent for a second, but I quickly recover. "What is it?"

"Do you know where the lookout tower is?"

"The lookout tower?" I echo vacantly. He's looking at me so intensely that it feels like my brain has stopped working. Who *is* he?

"According to the internet, there's a lookout tower around here somewhere. And I'd like to take some photos." He points at the camera that's hanging on a strap around his neck.

"Okay." I try to hold his gaze, but I lose this game. His stare is *too* intense.

"The tower is in the woods." I've found my voice again. "It's best to take this road and . . ."

I briefly give him directions as dozens of questions flash through my mind.

Who is he? What's he doing in our town? Is he just a tourist, or am I going to see him again?

"And that's where you'll find the tower," I say, ending my explanation.

"Thank you." The boy holds out his hand. "Um . . . ?"

"Maria." I quickly take his hand. It feels soft.

"Nice to meet you, Maria," he says. "I'm Cody."

MARIA & FERRIS

"Hey, Mom."

The second I hear Ferris's voice in the hallway, I forget all about Cody. I shoot upright on the couch.

"Come on in. Get inside. Quickly. It's pouring down. It's so good to see you again."

Ferris laughs. "Mom, you're crushing me."

"Am I not allowed to give my son a little cuddle?"

"Of course you are."

I look at the coffee table, laid out with a tablecloth. It's the old white one that I haven't seen for years. When we were little, Ferris and I stenciled red strawberries all over it.

I still remember that I wanted to print something else, not strawberries, but Ferris won the argument. As always. What *he* wanted happened. Because if I didn't go along with it, the resulting tantrum was way worse than me not getting my way.

"Maria bought cake, your favorite. You still like strawberry shortcake, don't you?"

"Love it."

"It's waiting for you in the living room. Give me your stuff. We don't want you having to lug your bag around. Peter, will you take it upstairs?"

I hear my dad mumbling in agreement. And then the door opens.

For the first time in months, I see my brother walking into the living room. First I see his bright yellow sneakers, his faded jeans, and a yellow hoodie with a busy black design on it. Then I see Ferris's little beard, his nose piercing, and his eyes.

His eyes, which look black but are actually bright blue, just like mine.

He's got a buzz cut, as if he's come straight from boot camp.

"Ah, little sis . . ." Ferris looks at me. "Fancy seeing you here."

"Yeah," I say with someone else's voice. "Me. Here."

"Don't I get a hug?" Ferris's voice is so strong and clear that it's scary. He's changed since the last time I saw him. That was when he'd just started at the center. Mom and Dad had insisted that I go with them.

Ferris sat in the visitors' room like a broken heap of misery. Some of the other boys watched him constantly. My mom noticed them too.

"Are you making friends here?" she'd asked.

"Loads" had been his reply.

I was sure he had a tough time there. So tough that I almost felt sorry for him.

Almost.

Because he was exactly where he belonged: far away from us.

After that, I always found an excuse so I wouldn't have

to go to visiting hours. Excuses in which Pip played a major role.

We had to do homework. I'd been invited to go see a play. It was her birthday.

If Pip knew how many times I'd used her as an excuse . . .

"I'll make coffee," Mom calls from the kitchen.

"Come on, little sis." Ferris opens his arms wide. "Just one little hug."

My dad comes into the living room. He glances at Ferris, who is waiting with outspread arms.

Then Dad looks at me. I can almost hear him thinking, *Stop being so difficult, Maria. Give Ferris a hug and get it over and done with.*

I get up and walk over to my brother, heart pounding.

It feels like I'm about to hug a wild animal.

Ferris wraps his arms around me like two steel cables.

He's gotten even more muscular than before, if that's possible.

"Missed you," says Ferris.

He obviously doesn't mean it, but he sounds so sincere that I almost start to doubt myself.

Almost.

"We're going to have such a great summer," he says, but then he adds in a whisper, "It could be your last."

We're going to have such a great summer. It could be your last . . .

I can barely get the strawberry shortcake down my throat.

The cream suddenly feels like cement sticking to the roof of my mouth. I even choke on the crumbly base.

When he's finished his cake, Ferris jumps up from the couch. "I'll clear this away, Mom."

"Really?" She looks at him in surprise. "That center's done you some good, huh?"

"It's a great place," Ferris says, nodding. "If you can call a place great when it's a prison."

The word "prison" is followed by silence.

The center is not officially a prison but an institution for troubled youth. A private clinic where young people receive therapy almost every day.

When Mom and Dad told him where he was going, he exploded. I don't think I've ever heard Ferris yell that loud.

But the alternative was an actual prison, and I think he was even more afraid of that.

"Fer—" Dad begins.

"I mean it," Ferris says. "The center really is okay. A room to myself, working out every day, people who cook for you. And you don't need to wonder who's crazy in there."

His gaze rests on me for a moment.

"Because everyone is."

More silence.

It's so painful this time that I forget how to breathe.

What a great idea, Mom. Yeah, an awesome idea to bring Ferris home for the summer.

"Will you help me?" Ferris asks me.

"Me?"

"I'll wash, and you can dry." Ferris takes the plates from the coffee table and carries them to the kitchen.

Washing up?

"We've got a dishwasher for that, haven't we?" I blurt.

"Not at the center," Ferris shouts from the kitchen. "I don't want to get too used to this luxury."

"Oh, just give the boy a hand." My mom makes a dismissive gesture. "He shouldn't have to do everything on his own."

With all the strength I have in me, I push myself off the couch.

Being alone in the kitchen with Ferris is not what I had in mind. He comes with the same set of instructions as Norah: *Stay as far away as possible.*

When I go into the kitchen, Ferris is already standing at the sink. He slides the four plates off the counter and into the water.

"Here." Ferris throws a dishcloth my way.

Silently we stand next to each other.

We're going to have such a great summer. It could be your last . . .

Why would Ferris say something like that? What's he planning?

I give my brother a sidelong glance. We have the same sharp nose and bone structure. I think you could lay our X-rays on top of each other and they'd match perfectly.

For as long as I can remember, people have told us we're so similar.

That hurts, because I'm not like Ferris. Never have been.

I never squashed bugs in the garden so I could watch them burst.

I never hid in the closet so I could creep up to his bed in the middle of the night and give him nightmares for months.

I never lost my mind when Dad came home with the wrong kind of salami.

And I have *never* hit Ferris.

"Help me, then." Ferris puts a wet plate on the counter. If I'm going to help him, I'll have to stand right up close. I take a deep breath and step forward.

Ferris washes the other three plates, and then it's the cake knife's turn.

He goes on rubbing the brush furiously over the blade, even long after it's clean.

I look at the sharp steel edge, and it seems to become even quieter in the kitchen.

Ferris takes the knife out of the soapy water and points it at me.

It could be your last . . .

It could be your last . . .

It could be your last . . .

He is going to stab me. I wait for the fierce flash of pain.

As long as it's quick, as long as I don't suffer too much . . .

"Maria?"

The pain doesn't happen.

I look at Ferris, still standing there with the cake knife in his hand.

"Are you going to dry it? Or not?"

I realize now that I've been holding my breath.

"Yeah." I quickly take a gulp of oxygen. "Sure."

MARIA & MYSTERY GUEST

have to get away from the house.

Away from my brother, away from my mom and dad, away from the minefield.

Without thinking about where I'm headed, I close the front door behind me.

We're going to have such a great summer. It could be your last . . .

Ferris has only been home for an hour, and I've already received my first death threat. Has he gone completely crazy?

But on the other hand, what was I expecting?

That he'd seriously be happy to see me?

Maybe I should go back and tell Mom and Dad what Ferris said. But what if they just stand up for him again?

Mom will defend Ferris and say that he's just struggling with being back home. And that I have to understand that he feels like an outsider after being away for months.

And Dad? He'll take Mom's side, as always.

As I reach the end of the street, my phone buzzes.

Probably Pip, asking when we're going to see each other again.

But can I tell her what Ferris did?

What if she tells her mom and dad, and they turn up on our doorstep?

I take my phone out of my pocket. It isn't Pip at all. It's Mystery Guest.

That's all. No time, no further instructions.

This must be the place for the second game.

I look at the map. The pin is in the woods again but in a different place.

When I look closer, I smile, because this is exactly the place where deep down I wanted to go.

The lookout tower rises far above the trees. When I tilt back my head, I can make out the top. Is Cody still there? I can't see any movement up on the tower.

Behind me, something rustles.

I turn around, but I can't see anyone. Probably nothing there.

And yet . . . I think that, out of the corner of my eye, I see a shadow darting away. Is MG watching me from the bushes?

"Hello?" My voice echoes through the silent trees. I stand there for a few seconds, looking in the direction the noise came from, but nothing else happens.

No cracking twigs, no sound of breathing, no shadows, nothing. The silence of the woods almost hurts my ears.

Most likely just an animal. This place is crawling with deer, and my dad says he even spotted a coyote when he was out for a morning walk.

I stand at the foot of the tower, looking up again, and then I grab the steel handrail. I take the first steps slowly but soon speed up.

My footsteps thud on the metal. Through the gaps in the steps, I can see the drop beneath my feet.

Heights have never been my thing, even though I did once think about jumping from this tower.

I told Pip about it recently. In my imagination, I was already standing on the edge.

And now here I am, racing to the top. This new challenge is helping me put my brother out of my mind for a while.

It could be your last . . .

Nearly there. Just another few steps and . . .

The view from the top is amazing. You can see for miles around. In all the years we've lived here, I've never been all the way to the top.

Ferris dared me to go up there with him last year, but no way. I could still remember climbing the Eiffel Tower in Paris with him, when he pretended he was going to push me over the railing.

He just laughed at me when I started screaming.

Strangely enough, I'm really enjoying the panoramic view from up here now.

I'm on my own, so nothing can go wrong. I look out at the tops of the trees in the bright sunlight, their leaves still wet from the recent rain.

The weather pays no attention to the forecasts.

The lake, Pip's and my lake, is gleaming, as if thousands of fireflies are circling above it.

In the distance are the highway and the racing traffic, the wind turbines, and the endless fields full of cows.

But no Cody. I feel a stab of disappointment, but that soon disappears when I spot an envelope hanging from the railing.

It's attached with a piece of tape and looks like it's about to blow away.

I snatch the envelope from the railing and open it. This time there aren't many words on the card, but they're still enough to give me goose bumps.

> Welcome to the second game.
> Stand on the railing for three minutes—
> and send me the video.

On the railing? I stare at the steel, which looks so slippery after the rain.

As I think back to the Eiffel Tower, a terrible thought occurs to me.

What if Ferris is behind this message? What if my brother wants me to fall to my death?

We're going to have such a great summer. It could be your last . . .

What if he said that because he knew what my next challenge would be?

When I look over the edge, my stomach flips.

It's insane that I ever even thought about jumping. I'm certain now that I'd never have dared to do it.

Who is telling me to do this? Why would I stand up there? Drinking a bottle of some unknown liquid is one thing, but *this*?

MARIA:

Are you out of your mind?

MYSTERY GUEST:

Are you quitting the game?

MG seems so calm that it makes me furious.

I look at the railing again. It's flat on top, like a wide balance beam.

I'm wearing sneakers today with ribbed soles.

Do the soles have enough grip?

I shake my head. Am I seriously considering this?

My phone buzzes again.

MYSTERY GUEST:

It'd be too bad if you stopped . . .

MARIA:

You'd find another victim, wouldn't you?

48

For a moment, an image of Pip flashes into my head again, but I push it away. She was there when I received the message by the lake, and she hadn't even touched her phone.

Had she?

They only answer when they want to. It's so annoying. It makes me want to throw my phone from the top of the tower.

But I want you. I like you.

I have no idea who's sending this, but that last sentence still echoes inside my mind like the final note at a concert.

Ferris is Mom's favorite. Mom is Dad's.

No one at home sees how Ferris treats me. No one at home sees me. But Mystery Guest does.

I look back at the drop. How would it feel to brave that height?

Like, maybe a thousand times hotter than this afternoon's spicy liquid . . .

Anyway, I said to Pip that I hoped things would get scary. Isn't this exactly what I wanted? To be in danger?

So that I can forget Ferris for a moment?

I position my phone at an angle on the railing, pointing the camera at myself. When I press the record button, the timer starts.

Three minutes.

The length of one song.

I take a deep breath and pull myself up onto the railing. The steel feels cold under my hands, and when my knee touches the metal, I feel dizzy.

The ground is so far away that it makes me nauseous.

What am I doing?

"Playing a game," I snap at myself. Then I pull my other knee onto the flat surface, and very slowly, I stand up.

My legs are trembling like crazy.

"Come on," I whisper. "You can do this."

It's no different from stand-up paddleboarding, which Pip and I tried the other week. We rented boards at a nearby lake.

We both tried to stand on the boards, but it was almost impossible. On my third attempt, my board flipped over, and I ended up in the water.

When I resurfaced, Pip's laughter was ringing out across the lake.

But if I fall now, she won't be laughing.

If I fall now, she can bury me.

I try not to look down as I slowly straighten my legs. And then, suddenly, I'm standing.

I'm *standing* on the railing.

All of my pores burst open. I feel the wind brushing against my body like a caress. Somewhere nearby a bird is singing. The sun is high in the sky, warming my face.

With my arms out, I try to keep my balance. I mustn't start swaying.

I fix my gaze on the horizon. *Don't look at the wind turbines, because they're turning. Always look for a fixed point.* That turned out to help with the paddleboarding too. After five failed attempts, Pip and I both managed to stay on our feet. We felt invincible.

But this is so much better.

I've never been this close to death, but strangely it's making me feel immortal.

If Ferris really is behind this, he'll be devastated to see me standing here, upright, completely chill.

Too bad, Ferris. You'll have to come up with something better if you want to beat me.

Just then, I hear a voice behind me, one I'd recognize anywhere.

"What the hell are you doing?"

MARIA & NORAH

Norah!

My sneakers slip. I flail my arms frantically to keep my footing.

I'm about to jump back onto the tower, but Norah is already behind me.

Yep, Pip's ex. If she reaches out her hands now . . .

"Norah . . ." My voice is almost lost in the wind.

Was it really blowing this hard just now?

"Maria . . ." I can't see her face, but I can *hear* the grin in her voice. "So you're finally going to commit suicide, huh?"

I try to look over my shoulder, but that just makes me sway again.

Norah has spotted my phone. She grabs it from the railing. "Wow. Are you filming yourself?"

"No." My answer comes way too quickly.

"Holy shit. You're going to film your suicide?"

"I'm not committing suicide!" I try to turn toward her, but one of my sneakers slips off the railing.

"Hey!" Norah grabs my shirt. "Don't fall yet."

She pulls me back onto the railing. My heart is about to explode.

If she hadn't grabbed me, I'd have fallen to my death.

"Did I just save your life?"

Norah is still holding on to my shirt. "Looks like you owe me, don't you think?"

I want to reply, but my voice isn't working. I have to get off the railing right now.

"Now that we're here . . ." As always, Norah's tone is clipped and businesslike. "We might as well have a chat."

I swallow hard, because I know what she wants to talk about. It's always about Pip, ever since the first time Norah and I met.

"How are things between the two of you?"

What am I supposed to say? I know any answer I give is going to make her mad.

"I *asked*"—Norah pushes her fist against my back while still holding on to my shirt. My upper body tilts forward. I'm staring death in the eyes—"how things are going."

"G-good," I say quickly. "They're going good."

"That's nice." Norah pushes me a little more. She's a female version of Ferris, and at least as dangerous.

"Don't do that." I hate the sound of despair in my voice, but I can't help it. Norah literally has my life in her hands. The toes of my sneakers are already over the edge, and it feels like my shirt is about to rip.

"Please pull me back," I beg her. "Please! Norah, I—"

"Let Pip go."

"Wh-what?"

"Let her go. Break up with her."

"But—"

"I don't care how you do it, but I want you to dump her. Today."

"But I . . ." *Need her.*

"You hurt her. You know that, right?"

Hurt her? What's she talking about?!

"When you told her she was *safe*."

"How . . . how do you know about that?"

"We talk. Didn't she tell you that?"

I gasp for breath.

"Hey, you know you're pretty heavy?"

I sink a little deeper. The ground is pulling on me like a magnet, as if it can't wait to have me.

"That's a long way down, Maria."

"Please pull me back up." I hear my shirt tearing. "Please. I'll do anything you ask. I'll—"

"Anything?"

I have no choice. I need to survive. I don't want to die for a long time yet.

"I'll break up with Pip," I say. "I swear!"

Those seem to be the magic words, because in one movement, Norah pulls me back.

I fall onto the wooden decking, clutching my chest with both hands, as if my heart is about to fall out.

Norah grabs my phone and stops the recording.

"We'll just delete this, then." She presses a few keys before tossing my phone into my lap. Then she walks to the stairs and looks back at me.

As always, her blond curls fall perfectly around her face, and her lips are painted red. She looks like some cutie from a 1950s commercial, but she's a wolf in sheep's clothing.

"It's been fun."

PIP

I was mad because she dumped me.
I couldn't live without her. I . . .

CODY

Why did I do it?
I just wanted to know what it would feel like.

NORAH

Maria got what she deserved.
She took Pip away from me.
I should have done it way sooner.

MARIA & MYSTERY GUEST

MARIA:

I played the second game.

MYSTERY GUEST:

I don't see a video.

MARIA:

Someone deleted it.

MYSTERY GUEST:

Then make another one.

MARIA:

No way. I nearly died!

MYSTERY GUEST:

So you're quitting?

Are they even reading what I'm saying?!

I slump onto the bottom step of the lookout tower and gaze ahead.

What if my shirt hadn't been strong enough? What if it had torn? I'd be lying here among the pine needles in a pool of blood.

I look at MG's question. Am I quitting? Well, there's no way I am ever, ever going to stand at that kind of height again.

MARIA:
So it seems.

MYSTERY GUEST:
Too bad.

MARIA:
Is that all you have to say?

MYSTERY GUEST:
Let's hope so. For your sake.

MARIA:
What do you mean?

MYSTERY GUEST:
If I say more, you'll be in deep trouble.

What is this about? I'm just about to ask, but then someone says my name.

"Maria?"

MARIA & CODY

I'm startled to see Cody emerge from the bushes.

Where did he come from?

Cody still has his camera around his neck. Cautiously he approaches me. "Maria? That's your name, right? You okay?"

I suddenly realize what I must look like. Red face, sweaty, windblown hair, mascara running down my cheeks . . .

"No," I say, giving him an honest reply. I put my phone back in my pocket and stand up. "I'm not okay."

"What's wrong?"

I look back at the tower. "Long story."

"I have plenty of time," Cody says with a big grin. One of his canine teeth is a little crooked, an imperfection in his otherwise perfect smile. "It's not like there's anything else going on around here, is there?"

Cody is playing with the spoon for his cappuccino, balancing it on his index finger.

We're sitting at a table on a corner outside the café. Most of the other tables are empty.

"So, are you going to tell me your long story?" Cody has taken off his baseball cap. I can see his eyes even better now. He has bushy eyebrows and tanned skin, as if he's spent long days outside in the sunshine.

His white T-shirt is gently billowing in the breeze, and I notice again how handsome he is.

"I don't know where to start," I say.

"At the beginning?"

I hesitate. I don't know this guy at all. Should I really pour my heart out to him?

But maybe it's a good thing that I don't know him. Maybe he won't instantly disapprove of MG the way Pip did.

"I got these messages from someone who calls themself Mystery Guest," I say. "Some stranger in a mask."

Cody takes a sip of cappuccino, and a bit of foam clings to his top lip. "And what do they want from you?"

"To play a game."

"And what exactly does that involve?"

"I have to carry out challenges. Dangerous ones," I say. I shiver as I remember what happened on the tower. If Norah had let go of me, I wouldn't be sitting here now.

She saved me.

But why?

She could have let me fall to my death, and no one would have known I didn't jump.

I climbed up onto the railing myself!

Or does she just want to see me suffer when I lose Pip?

Pip . . .

The thought of having to break up with her makes my stomach lurch.

If I don't, Norah might still do something to hurt me. Like Ferris, she's crazy enough.

The way she laughed when she had my life in her hands . . .

She was enjoying it!

I stir my tea. The honey melted long ago, but the tapping sound of the spoon against the glass calms me down.

Can't say the same for Pip. It always drives her—

"Could you stop that noise?" Cody's voice is loud as he puts his hand on mine. "It's getting on my nerves."

I smile. "My girlfriend can't stand it either."

"Yeah, a lot of people can't. It's so irritating." Cody looks at me. "But anyway, you were talking about dangerous challenges. What exactly do you have to do?"

"Drink weird concoctions, stand on a railing."

There's silence for a moment, but then Cody's eyes widen.

"The railing at the top of the lookout tower?!"

I nod.

"And you actually did that?"

"Yeah."

Now he's going to tell me I'm crazy, like Pip did.

"What did it feel like?"

I look up in surprise. Is that seriously Cody's first question?

"Well . . ." I think about the moment before Norah arrived. The feeling of the wind on my cheeks, the birdsong in my ears.

"It felt . . . unbeatable."

"I can imagine." Cody gazes ahead with a dreamy expression on his face. "The kind of moment when you finally feel that you're really alive."

"Exactly," I say in surprise. "Do you know that feeling?"

"I sometimes deliberately do dangerous things, just to get that kick," says Cody. The look on his face shifts from dreamy to dark, and I don't dare ask any more questions.

What exactly does he mean?

"It's too bad that the unbeatable feeling always fades away so quickly," he says. "And then you have to chase the thrill again."

We order two grilled sandwiches after the drinks, and Cody shows me some photos on his camera. Pictures of the beach, of clouds, and of children playing.

"That's my little brother," he says, pointing at a boy.

"Really?" I look closer, but I can't see any resemblance.

"He has a different dad," says Cody.

"How about your dad? What's he like?"

Cody doesn't reply, just moves on to the next photo. All kinds of things flash past, from a bunch of dogs to a fairground.

Doesn't he want to talk about his dad?

"Where do you come from?" I ask.

"It's not about where I'm from," he says. "It's about where I am *now*. And right now, I'm with you."

"That's kind of profound," I say.

I remember the message that Mystery Guest sent me.

Isn't that what life's all about? Knowing who you can trust and who you can't?

Cody's philosophical way of talking sounds kind of similar . . .

I study him from the side. His bottom lip is plumper than his top one, and he's biting it in concentration.

Could he be Mystery Guest?

After all, he did appear just after the messages began . . .

Is that a coincidence? Or am I sitting with the person who's been threatening me, the person who says it's a good thing they're keeping their mouth shut and I'll regret it if they don't?

"These are from my trip to France." Cody shows me some more photos. "I went backpacking with my cousin."

I look at the photos of a rickety old van and some views.

If he's Mystery Guest, he's very good at hiding it. When I told him about the lookout tower, he seemed genuinely shocked.

I don't want it to be him.

Because if it's him, we can never be friends.

And if I lose Pip, I'm going to need a friend.

"Are you staying?" I ask him.

Cody looks at me. "Where? Here in town?"

"Yeah."

"Would you like me to?"

"Yes," I admit. "I'd like that."

"Then I'll stay. At least for now, until it gets too boring."

A car stops in front of the café. When I see the shade of red paint, my stomach flips.

What's Mike doing here?

Mike stares at me but doesn't say anything.

"Who's that?" I hear Cody ask the question, but I can't answer.

I see the café owner looking our way.

What is Mike up to? He knows the whole town hates him, doesn't he? So why is he following me?

"Who's that?" I hear Cody ask again. "A friend of yours?"

Ab-so-lute-ly not.

What if Mike *is* Mystery Guest?

I think back to the last message. Suddenly I'm not so sure I can rule Mike out.

He turned up during the first challenge, he'd be crazy enough to make me stand on the railing, and he wouldn't be sorry if I fell to my death.

He thinks I ruined *his* life, so maybe now he's doing the same to mine.

Then Mike steps on the gas and disappears from sight.

MARIA & MIKE

There are two options for the way home: through the town itself or through the farmland.

I go for the second one and walk along the road and past fields of crops.

Cody . . .

My head is full of the new boy. I want to see him again.

I hear the sound behind me too late. Way too late.

When I turn and see the red convertible, I have nowhere to escape.

Mike pulls up beside me and opens the passenger door.

"Get in" is all he says.

I look around, but there's no one in sight.

In the distance, there's a farmer on a tractor, but he won't hear me if I call for help.

"No," I say. "I am not getting in."

Mike pulls out a knife. It's small, but it looks as sharp as a razor.

"It wasn't a question, Maria."

✳ ✳ ✳

We tear along the asphalt road that leads out of town. Where is Mike taking me? What is he planning?

"Who was that loser you were sitting with outside the café?" asks Mike.

"C-Cody," I say. "He's new."

"Ah, fresh meat." Mike glances over at me. I feel his gaze burning through my shirt. He's probably looking at my breasts, just like he did that night.

I dig my nails into the palms of my hands. To my surprise, we don't take the turn for the highway. Mike drives on past the fields.

"Where . . . where are we going?"

"That's for me to know and you to find out." Mike turns his eyes back to the road. "How are you doing? I heard your brother's back home."

We're going to have such a great summer. It could be your last . . .

"Yep."

"And how's that going?"

I don't reply, just look at the passing landscape. The first time I rode in Mike's convertible, I thought it was awesome, but now the wind is way too annoying. I wish he'd drive a bit more slowly, but there's no way I'm going to ask him to do that.

"Is he your boyfriend? That Cody guy? Or are you still together with Tip?"

"Pip," I correct him. "Yeah, we're still together."

For now, I think.

Mike steps on the gas again. For the first time, I dare to take a good look at him, at his sharp jawline and his stubble, at his blue-gray eyes, at his bleached blond hair. It's grown out quite a lot. There's about an inch of dark hair at the roots.

"Are you checking me out, Maria?"

"No." I quickly look straight ahead.

"That's a good thing," says Mike. "Because the last time we played that game, I didn't end up liking it much."

After driving for about fifteen minutes, Mike finally pulls the car over. We haven't driven anywhere in particular. We're just parked up next to some field or another.

There are cows behind the fence, staring at us in surprise. I bet no one ever stops here.

I see the highway in the distance and the power cables drawing lines across the landscape.

"Okay." Mike switches off the engine and turns to me.

"This seems like a good place for us to have our conversation."

I look at the passenger door. If I'm fast, I can get away. But what then? Mike would soon catch up with me in his car. And then there's his knife . . .

"Do you recognize this place?"

I shake my head.

"You don't? I'm disappointed in you." Mike leans one hand on the steering wheel, the other on the headrest behind me. "I thought you were kind of obsessed with her."

"Who?"

Mike ignores my question and rubs his cheeks. It makes an annoying, rasping sound.

"You just moved on with your life, didn't you?" Mike looks at me.

"What was I supposed to do?"

"Stand still, just like me."

"I didn't do anything wrong."

"If you say so."

The weird feeling in my stomach grows. "What . . . what are we doing here?"

"Talking."

"I don't know if I want to."

"Why not? We can talk about Tip."

"Pip," I say, correcting him again. "Why should we talk about her?"

"Or about that Cody. Does he know what you're like? Maybe I should warn him about what you do to guys."

My breath catches in my throat. There's no one who can hear us. Maybe I should record our conversation as evidence? But if I take my phone out now, Mike will know what I'm up to.

Mike may be a creep, but he's not stupid.

When you've been the local drug dealer for years without getting caught, you clearly have enough brains to stay out of trouble.

"Cody and I are just friends," I say.

"We both know you can't make regular friends." Mike lowers his right hand slightly and grabs one of my curls. He winds my hair around his finger before letting it go.

"Don't do that," I say.

70

"Don't do what? This?" Mike takes another strand of hair. My whole body is covered in goose bumps.

I should never have gone home through the farmland.

I should have taken the road through town.

"This is exactly what you wanted that night at Outcast, isn't it? For me to touch you like this?" Mike takes another lock of hair in his hand, then leans forward. Is he seriously going to kiss me?

"So why were you like that afterward? So . . . *difficult*?" As he says that last word, he tugs my head back in one movement.

"Ow!" I shriek. "Stop it!"

"Stop what?" Mike hisses the words in my ear. "This?"

And then he pulls me to one side. I fall against him, clawing at his hands in an attempt to break free.

There's no point. He literally has me in his grip.

"Ow . . ." I feel the tears filling my eyes. "Mike, I . . ."

"Begging won't help you, Maria." Mike pulls harder. My head is almost in his lap now. It feels like my skull is breaking open. It hurts so much.

I kick out, try to hit his face with my fist, but I just graze his stubbly cheek, and Mike chuckles.

"It feels good, seeing you struggle like that."

I've got to get out of here.

I hit the horn. The sound echoes across the empty fields.

"Stop that," Mike growls, but I manage to press the horn one more time. Longer this time, maybe five seconds.

Someone's going to react, aren't they? A curious farmer, a concerned cyclist?

"I said, *Stop it!*" Mike gives me a shove, and I fall back into my seat, whacking the door with my elbow.

It hurts, but I'm more relieved to be free.

Without stopping to think, I grab the door handle.

Mike probably locked the door, but I can climb out. I have to get away.

"Hey!" Mike grabs me again, and I feel the sharp blade of the knife against my throat. "You. Stay. Here."

"M-Mike . . ." I gasp for breath.

"Sit down," he says.

"Yeah, yeah, yeah. I'm sitting! Put that knife away!"

Slowly Mike lowers the knife. I'm panting, like I've just run a long way. Mike cracks his knuckles.

I can't get away. Mike has me completely in his power.

The silence that follows lasts so long that I've caught my breath again by the time Mike speaks.

"This is where Shannon was found," I hear him say.

Shannon?

Why has Mike suddenly started talking about *her*?

And how does he know she was found here? The exact location was never revealed. The news reports just said it was in a field.

And there are plenty of those around here.

Pip and I rode our bikes for miles, looking for clues, but we didn't find anything.

"My dad was part of the search team," Mike says. "He was the one who found her. Did you know that?"

No, of course I didn't know that.

My scalp is stinging and throbbing.

"It still gives him nightmares," Mike says. "He sees her lying there, half naked in the grass. I'm going to hear him screaming in his sleep again these next few weeks."

I try to imagine the crime scene. Lots of details were released. There were photos online of the clothes she was wearing that night. A leather jacket, a black skirt, red tights, gray panties, and a bra . . .

"Shan . . . non!" Mike closes his eyes and puts on a tortured expression. For a moment, I see the resemblance to his father. "That's how he says it: 'Shan-non . . .'"

"Stop . . ." I say. Saying her name like that, in this place, feels disrespectful. As if we're making fun of her.

"Why should I stop?" Mike sniffs. "You had no problem mentioning her name when you hounded me out of town, did you? 'It was just like with Shannon!' That was what you said, wasn't it?"

He's seriously disturbed.

Why are there so many crazy people living around here?

Ferris, Norah, *him* . . .

I grab the door handle and practically fall out of the car. He didn't lock the door after all!

I have to get away as fast as I can. I don't care how long it takes me to walk back home. I'm not staying here a second longer.

"Say her name! I dare you," Mike shouts after me. "Shannon!"

MARIA & PIP

"So Mike *kidnapped* you?!" Pip is lying on her bed with Jax on her stomach.

"Yeah." I take a deep breath. "He showed me the place where Shannon was found."

Pip gasps. "Seriously? How does he know where it is?"

"Apparently his dad found her."

"Wow . . ."

"Yep, you can say that again. Seems he's still having nightmares about it, and he screams her name."

"Mr. Swan?"

I picture the tough farmer with his huge hands. He's like a block of cement with arms and legs.

"The crime scene must have been really bad."

"Yeah, I guess." Pip's gaze wanders as she slowly strokes Jax's fur.

I know I need to break up with her, but how am I supposed to do that? Pip and I have been together almost constantly for months. I wouldn't even know how to function without her now.

"How did it go with Ferris?" Pip asks. "Did you survive the first day?"

"Barely. He threatened me when we were doing the dishes."

"You serious?" Pip sits up a bit. Jax hops onto the floor. "What did he say?"

"Nothing. Never mind." I look outside. The lampposts cast patches of yellow on the street. In a few minutes, Pip's dad will come tell me that it really is time for me to go home.

"You scared of him?"

"Yes."

"Come here." Pip puts her arm around me and kisses my shoulder. She'll never do that again after I say the words that have been haunting my mind all afternoon.

I can keep chewing away on them like gum, but sooner or later, they're going to have to come out.

I take a deep breath, but Pip speaks first.

"It's a good thing you had some distraction from Ferris today." Pip's lips rest on my shoulder for a moment. "I heard you were sitting outside the café with a boy?"

I look at her. "How do you know that?"

"We live in a town with less than two thousand inhabitants," says Pip. "You really think you could sit there with no one noticing?"

I don't reply.

"Who is he?"

"Cody," I say. "He's new around here, no big deal."

That's not true. Cody certainly is a big deal. But it doesn't seem like a good idea to say that out loud right now.

"How do you know him?"

"I just ran into him. He's here to take photos."

"Photos . . ." Pip frowns. "Is that the only reason he's here? You sure he's not here because of you?"

"Why would he be here because of me?" But the thought of that makes me feel warm. I can't help it.

"Because you're beautiful?" Pip kisses me again, this time on my neck. "But he's not going to have you. You're already mine."

I close my eyes and feel Pip's lips on my skin, a feeling that, in a few minutes' time, I'll never know again.

But if I don't do this, Norah will know where to find me. And I don't want to think about what she'll do to me. She'll destroy me again, but in a different way.

"Pip?" I take a deep breath. "I actually wanted to talk to you."

Pip just goes on kissing me, from my throat to my ears.

Her lips kiss each of my earrings, then my cheek, the corner of my mouth.

"Pip . . ." I sit up. "I'm serious."

"What's wrong?"

"I . . ." I've been thinking all day about how to say this, but I know there's no good way to do it. Maybe it would be best to rip the bandage off in one go.

Painful but fast.

"I want to break up with you."

As soon as the words leave my mouth, I know this wasn't the right way. I should have picked at the edges of the bandage and pulled it away very slowly, one hair at a time.

But now it's too late.

"You want to *break up* with me?"

It sounds so much worse coming from Pip's mouth.

"Yes."

"Cody . . ." whispers Pip. "He's your new plaything, right?"

"No," I say quickly. "No way."

"What does he have that I don't?" Pip's eyes fill with tears.

"This isn't about Cody. I . . ."

"What does he kiss like?"

"What?" I shake my head. "We haven't kissed!"

Jax slinks under the desk, as if he's trying to hide from what's about to happen.

But Pip doesn't start a fight, not even now. She stands up, goes to sit in her desk chair. Picks up her phone—and doesn't say anything.

"Pip . . ." I begin.

"Just go," she says quietly.

I want to tell her about Norah, but it won't make any difference. "Over" means "over."

Pip's bedroom door opens.

"Maria, it's late and . . ." Pip's dad falls silent. "Everything okay?"

"Great," I reply, but it sounds sarcastic. "I was just about to leave."

I glance at Pip, but she's scrolling on her phone and doesn't say anything.

I look up at Pip's window. The light behind her curtains goes off. She doesn't peek outside. When I check my phone, I see that she's offline.

All those months together, all gone in one instant.

Since I found out what it feels like to have Pip, I've realized just how lonely I was before. I never let anyone come as close to me as Pip, and from now on, I'll have to do everything on my own again.

Unmask Mystery Guest, steer clear of Mike, and survive Ferris—all on my own.

The only good thing about all this is that Norah will finally leave me in peace.

I stare at Pip's curtains as if I can command them to open with the power of my mind.

Come on, I think. *Just take a quick look, even if it's just for a second.*

But she doesn't. Maybe she's already in bed.

Perhaps Pip really has become a bit harder, and I've become softer. Maybe we've both changed into each other, just a little bit.

At that moment, my phone buzzes. My heart leaps.

Is it Pip?

But then I see the mask on my screen: MG is back.

MARIA & MYSTERY GUEST

When I look at the pin on the map, I almost drop my phone.

Why do I have to go there?

Is this for the third game?

But why *there*?

I've avoided that place all this time, for good reason.

An ominous feeling comes over me: What if they *know*?

MARIA:

MYSTERY GUEST:

I look at the pin again. This isn't a bluff. They really do know something.

But what, exactly?

I think about this afternoon's messages. When MG said it would be better for me if they kept their mouth shut . . .

I look back up at Pip's curtains. What I really want to do is ring her doorbell and tell her everything. But that feels impossible now. I'm stuck in Norah's web. If I want to get rid of her, I'll lose Pip too. It's that simple.

From now on, I'll have to fight MG on my own, no matter how scary that is.

I need to find out who this is and shut their mouth once and for all.

Whatever they know about that place, it can't come out. Not ever.

I can find that spot even in the dark.

It's not far from Outcast, but there's a completely different atmosphere here. This is a piece of no-man's-land.

I hold up my phone and shine its light in front of me. There used to be an old church here, but it went up in flames in December of last year. Parts of the walls and roof are still standing, but it's all scorched black.

As I go closer, it's as if I can smell the stench of burning again. That's impossible. The fire was months ago, but still . . .

Why does MG want me to come here?

I look around, but I don't see anything out of the ordinary.

It's silent, just an owl hooting nearby.

I light up the ruins of the church. There's graffiti on the walls, but I can't read what it says.

The burning smell is in my nose again, and I'm flooded with memories. Memories that I wisely buried away in a deep, deep place.

Why am I still here?

The challenge was just to come here, and I've done that.

I'm about to turn to go home when I hear rustling in the bushes.

It's like the sound I heard at the lookout tower. I thought it was an animal then, but this time, I can see the branches moving wildly.

Someone is actually coming . . .

Is it Mystery Guest? Have they changed the rules of the game? Are they going to reveal themself already?

But why? What are they going to do?

I brace myself as someone steps out of the bushes.

I'm expecting to see that green mask, but it's something completely different.

For one moment, I relax, but at the sight of that yellow hoodie, my breath catches in my throat.

MARIA & FERRIS

"Hey, little sis." Ferris has his hood up, and strange shadows are falling over his face. He turns on his flashlight, aiming it at me.

"What . . ." I swallow the rest of my question because I know the answer. What's he doing here? *He* is Mystery Guest.

It's just as I feared when I had to climb onto the railing of the lookout tower.

Ferris made a fake profile, put on a mask, and sent me those challenges.

Why? To punish me? To see how far his little sis would go?

It must have made him feel so powerful, making me do exactly what he wanted me to.

"I wanted to see what kind of state the church was in," says Ferris.

He walks over to the ruin and easily pulls a loose brick from a wall.

"Crazy, huh?" He looks straight at me. "Being here again."

I look around. Can I get away? But Ferris clearly did a lot of working out when he was at the center. His muscles are bigger than ever, and he's probably faster too.

The thought of him catching up to me in the middle of the woods chills me.

"What . . . what are we doing here?"

"Well, I've come to soak up the atmosphere," Ferris says, sniffing. "I don't know what *you're* doing here."

I don't understand.

"You asked me to come here, didn't you?" I splutter.

"What are you talking about?" Ferris says with a frown. "I'm warning you. If you're about to start lying again, I'll kill you."

"But you sent me this location and . . ."

"I told you. Don't *lie*." Ferris throws the brick in my direction. It lands a few footsteps away, but I feel the dull thud all the way into my bones.

"It makes me mad when you lie." Ferris grabs another brick and takes a step toward me. "You know that, don't you?"

I nod. It's all I can do.

It's like I'm seven years old again, and Ferris has come into my room. One afternoon he swept all the stuff off my desk just because he'd had a bad day at school. A teacher had thrown him out of the classroom—and Ferris had gone berserk.

And it didn't stop when he got home. He was screaming at the top of his lungs. All that time (was it seconds or minutes?), I sat there, frozen, and let him do what he wanted.

I used to collect unicorns, and I saw my favorite one lying there, smashed among my schoolbooks.

84

He didn't leave my room until his voice finally became hoarse.

Mom came upstairs and went into Ferris's room, next door to mine.

I heard her soft voice and his deep voice. It took her a long time to calm him down. And then she went back downstairs.

She didn't even come and check on me, even though I was sure she'd heard the noise coming from my room.

"So for once, how about we don't lie, okay?" Ferris says now, tossing the brick from his right hand to his left hand and back again.

"Okay . . ." I say quietly, but I have no idea what's going on.

Is he the person behind the mask or not?

"Why didn't you come visit me at the center?"

I look up warily. "Because . . . because I had other . . . commitments."

"That's another *lie!*" Ferris throws the second brick at me. I have to jump out of the way, and it lands right in front of my feet. Some mud splashes up onto my pants.

"You were supposed to be honest," scoffs Ferris, "or there's no point to this conversation, is there?"

He grabs another brick from the dilapidated wall. This time he pulls out two, stuck together with a layer of cement.

"So I'm going to ask you one more time. Why didn't you come visit me?"

"I was scared, okay?" I look at Ferris's dark eyes under his hood.

"Scared of me?"

"Yes."

Apparently Ferris is satisfied with my answer, because he lowers the bricks a little.

"Did you think about me at all these past few months? While I was locked up inside that place?"

"Of course I did."

"And what exactly did you think?"

"That I . . ." I hesitate, because I'm afraid this is going to make him explode again. "That I was glad that you were locked up."

"And now that I'm home?" Ferris looks at me. "Are you scared again?"

"Yes."

"Why? I'd be more scared of—"

"How about we go home?" I say, interrupting him. "Please?"

"Why?" Ferris shakes his head. "I'm not ready to sleep yet, not by a long shot."

I remember all those nights when Ferris was awake at home. I could hear him working out in his bedroom. Endless repetitions, slamming weights up and down.

Mom and Dad said it was good for him, that he could get rid of some of his aggression that way, but it turned into an obsession. And his muscles grew bigger and bigger by the week. There was no way I could ever beat him in a fight.

Unless I was smarter than him. The only way I could defeat him was with my brain.

"Then let's talk some more at home," I suggest. Just as long as we get back to civilization, that's the most important thing. Somewhere he won't smash my skull with a couple of bricks.

"I have one more question." Ferris raises the bricks. "Do you *seriously* believe I started the fire that night?"

The woods are suddenly deathly silent. I can't even hear the owl anymore.

I look at the burned-out church. When I got here with my mom and dad, it stank so bad. Everything was soaked from the firefighters' hoses, and there were scorched beams and blackened bricks all over the ground.

"You were found guilty, Ferris," I say. "Why does it matter what I believe?"

Ferris smiles. "That's not an answer to my question."

"I think you were confused," I say. "And maybe you don't remember exactly what happened that night."

Ferris's eyebrows shoot up. "Are you serious?"

I remember the moment when Ferris got home. His eyes were wide with panic, and he collapsed into the coatrack in the hall. My mom and dad knew right away that he'd been using.

Drugs, probably from Mike.

"Do you *really* think I was so far gone that I wouldn't remember burning down a church?"

I look at my brother, who stopped being my brother long ago.

"Yeah, Ferris. That's what I think."

Ferris looks at the bricks in his hands. For a second, I think he's about to throw them at me anyway, but then he drops them among the other rubble.

"That is really screwed up, Maria." Ferris walks straight past me and disappears back into the bushes.

MARIA & MYSTERY GUEST

I stand there for a few minutes, trying to get my heartbeat under control.

Ferris is not Mystery Guest.

My brother may be many things, but he's not an actor.

When I mentioned the message, he genuinely had no idea what I was talking about. Mystery Guest clearly wanted me to meet my brother here. But why? So that the truth would come out?

Could MG know that my brother didn't start the fire?

I think back to that night in December, when I saw Ferris taking pills with his friends at Outcast.

Soon after that, there were plumes of smoke billowing above the woods.

When I saw the smoke, I quickly made a decision.

Ferris was completely out of it. He wouldn't remember anything about that night, maybe not even lighting a fire.

His aggressive attitude would be perfectly in line with

such reckless behavior. Any judge would believe me—and not him.

A terrible feeling spreads throughout my body.

What if Mystery Guest knows about my lie?

What if he knows I took advantage of Ferris's drug habit and behavior to make sure he *finally* ended up behind bars?

I grab my phone and quickly type a message.

MARIA:

Why did I have to come to this place?

MYSTERY GUEST:

To revisit some old memories. Did it work?

A weird thought hits me. What if MG sent my brother a message that he should come here too?

But why would Ferris listen to a stranger?

MARIA:

Why are you doing this?

MYSTERY GUEST is sending a photo.

I stare at the picture on my screen, but my brain barely registers what I'm looking at.

This is impossible.

There was no one around that night. I'm 1,000 percent certain of that, because I was extremely careful.

What did I miss?

How can this photograph exist?

MYSTERY GUEST:

Do I finally have your attention?

It's like a brick hitting me right in the stomach.

MARIA:

What do I have to do? I'll do anything. Just delete that photo. Okay?

MYSTERY GUEST:

Sleep tight and have a good rest.

We'll continue the game tomorrow.

AUGUST

SUMMER VACATION

PIP

You have to believe me when I say it happened on impulse.

I shouldn't have taken that knife with me, of course, but it was never my intention to kill her.

It really wasn't.

Oh, I . . .

I keep remembering how easily the blade slid into her chest.

It was so awful.

CODY

Drowning is apparently the least worst way to die, right?

NORAH

I should have pushed Maria off that tower when I had the chance.

It would have been way easier than strangling her.

MARIA & HER MOM AND DAD

"Did you sleep okay?" My mom looks up at me as she takes eight perfectly browned bread rolls out of the oven, just like we always used to have during vacation.

"Great."

I can hardly tell her I was awake half the night because I was afraid that Ferris was going to come into my room.

Having a good night's sleep with Ferris right next door is something I'll never be able to do again.

Eventually I did fall asleep, tumbling from one nightmare into another. Pip screaming at me, Norah pushing me from the tower, Mike crashing the convertible with me in the passenger seat, Ferris throwing that brick . . .

I woke up in a cold sweat.

The first thing I saw when I unlocked my phone was the photo Mystery Guest sent.

The photo that could change everything.

How *can* there be a photograph? I still don't get it. Who took a photograph of me from the bushes that night?

"Your brother's still in bed." Mom puts napkins on four plates. "He must be tired, what with the move from the center to here. It's obviously all about structure there. It's good that he got to blow off a bit of steam when he went out last night."

I nod. If she only knew where Ferris *really* was last night.

I still don't know why he came to the ruin.

To soak up the atmosphere, Ferris said, but why exactly at that moment? If he really did get a message from MG, I can't believe he'd actually do as he was told.

Ferris isn't going to do anything that could get him into trouble again. No way he's going to risk his freedom and have to stay months longer at the center.

But then why was he there? Because of me? Did he follow me from Pip's house? But why didn't I notice him?

I sit down at the table and take one of the bread rolls from the bowl.

"Will you wait a little longer?" Mom looks at me. "Ferris is still asleep."

"I know he is, but I'm hungry."

"We might as well start." Dad gives me a wink. "That boy's going to be in bed half the day, Suze. Before you know it, the bread will be cold."

Mom opens her mouth to say something, but when Dad takes a roll, she sits down.

For a moment, it feels like it should be: just the three of us.

Until Mom says, "Ferris wants to go out somewhere today. We thought a day at the beach might be nice."

I almost choke on my first bite. "The four of us?"

"We think it would be good to do something together," says Mom.

I look at my dad. "And you agree, do you?"

Dad takes another bite and then chews with exaggerated slowness. There's a crumb stuck to his top lip when he finally replies.

"We're a family, Maria."

That isn't an answer to my question, I think.

"And it'd be good to get used to the way things were again," my dad adds.

"Why? He's going to be in there for months, isn't he?"

Dad shakes his head. "Ferris is nearly done at the center now. He'll be allowed to come live with us from mid-September."

"What?" I shake my head. "How's that possible? He started a f—"

"We are aware of the facts. Thank you, Maria." Mom's voice sounds cold and formal. She takes a roll and slices it open. She does it far too roughly, making a mess of the roll and then shoving in a slice of cheese.

"Ferris's program was for ten months," says Dad. "You knew that, didn't you?"

"But the ten months aren't over yet, and they said it could be extended," I say. "By another six months."

"Ferris has shown good behavior, so they're letting him leave earlier."

Good behavior? I think about last night. What would the management at the center say if they heard that Ferris was throwing bricks at his sister?

"You've noticed he's changed too, haven't you?" Mom flattens her roll, and it cracks under her hand, scattering crumbs all over her plate. "He seems a lot calmer."

"That's right," I say. "He's only aggressive in private now."

"What do you mean?" Mom looks at me.

"He's threatening me," I say.

Mom looks shocked. "Threatening you? How?"

I glance over my shoulder. There's still no sign of Ferris. Should I tell them what happened last night?

But then I'd have to tell them what I was doing at the burned-out church.

What if my mom and dad start looking into the whole thing again and discover that something isn't right?

And then there's Mystery Guest's photo. What if that gets out?

"Maria?" Dad says. "What do you mean by 'he's threatening me'?"

I see the tense look on Mom's face. She doesn't want to hear what I have to say. She wants to believe in the fairy tale that the people at the center have told her. That her disturbed son can return to society because of his good behavior.

If I tell the truth now, it's going to be just the same as before. She'll choose his door—and walk straight past mine.

"It's nothing," I say. "Never mind."

"So you're just accusing him again?" Mom shakes her head. "You're not getting off that easily, young lady."

The tone of her voice makes me curl up inside.

"F-Ferris *is* guilty," I stammer. "The judge found him guilty."

"Yes, thanks to *your* statement."

"Suze . . ." Dad rests one hand on hers, but she pulls it away. Pushing back her chair, she stands up.

"You already destroyed your brother's life once," she snaps. "Wasn't that enough?"

MARIA & CODY

"Hey, Maria. Hang on a second."

In the center of town, Cody comes running up to me. His camera is around his neck, swinging back and forth with every step.

He's carrying a plastic bag with four croissants in it.

"Want one?"

I don't know what makes me happier: seeing him or the thought of a croissant.

"Please."

"Here you go." Cody takes a soggy croissant out of the bag, and I immediately sink my teeth into it.

"Hey, you're hungry." Cody takes a bite of his croissant, and we walk on together. "Don't they feed you at home?"

"We had a fight," I say. "I left the house without any break-fast."

"Ouch. What did you fight about?"

I look to one side, taking in his tanned skin and his green

baseball cap. There are small holes in his T-shirt, but it looks like he bought it like that. His pants are hanging low, the laces of his sneakers trailing on the ground.

"About my brother," I say. "He's back home this summer. He . . . he was away at a special center."

"Ah, okay." Cody's expression is suddenly serious.

"A place for young people with serious behavioral problems," I add. "He was allowed to come home on probationary release. To see how things would work out, but . . ."

"They're not working out," says Cody, completing my sentence for me.

"Exactly."

"Is he aggressive toward you?"

"Yeah, that's part of it."

"What else?"

"He threatened to kill me."

"Serious?" Cody stops and points at a bench where I've often sat with Pip. "Want to sit down?"

As we sit, my eyes automatically look across the street. The curtains are still closed at Shannon's mom and dad's house. As usual. I think her parents just want to disappear.

If *my* daughter got murdered, I'd probably move away.

All those stories, all those people staring . . .

Pip and I were two of those staring people. When we were really into Shannon's story, we used to sit on this bench almost every day so we could keep an eye on their front door.

I don't know what exactly we were hoping for. Maybe some new information?

But all we saw was the procession of mourners heading into the house with serious looks on their faces and coming back out with puffy eyes.

The whole town was in mourning.

"Who lives there?" asks Cody when he sees me looking.

"Shannon." I look at Cody, but he doesn't react to her name.

"Don't you know who she is?" I ask in surprise.

"No. Should I?"

Have I ever met anyone who doesn't know about her? Don't think so. "Shannon" is a household name, not just in our town, but for miles around.

It even ended up on the national news: *Teenage girl murdered and dumped in a field.*

"Don't you pay attention to the news? Social media?"

"I don't have a phone." Cody raises his hands. "Sorry."

"You don't have a phone?"

"Don't you know how harmful the radiation is? And how addictive those things are?"

"Yeah, but . . ."

"But you've never met anyone without a phone." With a grin, Cody takes a bite of his second croissant. "Well, it's nice to meet you."

Cody is becoming more and more mysterious. Who is this strange guy with a camera but no phone? What is he doing here? Is he really here just because of me?

"So, who is Shannon?" Cody says. "Tell me about her."

"Keep your voice down a bit," I say. "It's better not to say her name too loud. People freak out."

"Is she dead?" Cody guesses.

"Murdered," I reply.

"Did you know her well?"

"She was in the same year as my brother."

"Did he . . ." Cody pauses. "Did he have something to do with her death?"

I burst out laughing. "Nah."

But it's like Cody threw a glass of water in my face. I instantly wake up.

"Well, I don't know for sure," I continue. "They never caught the guy who did it."

"Whoa, nasty stuff."

"Yeah." I think about it. Could Ferris have had anything to do with Shannon? He was questioned at the time like Pip and me, but never seriously. Ferris isn't *that* crazy, is he?

"What exactly happened to her?"

"She went missing after a night out. A farmer found her later, out in the fields."

I think about Mike's dad. It must have been such an awful thing to see.

"She was half naked. The toxicology tests showed that there was a large dose of GHB in her blood."

Cody nods slowly. "The rape drug."

"Exactly. The creep raped her and then strangled her."

Cody swallows the last bit of his croissant and puts the empty bag in his pocket.

"There's a trash can over there," I say.

"It's plastic," says Cody. "You're supposed to separate it for recycling."

I smile. "You're a bit of a Goody Two-shoes, aren't you?"

"But I'm not wrong, am I?"

Cody pets a passing dog and has a quick chat with the owner.

"Is it a Welsh springer spaniel?" he asks.

The owner is surprised that he knows the breed.

"I love dogs," says Cody, giving the spaniel another scratch behind the ears.

When the dog has gone, Cody turns back to me.

"That guy yesterday . . . the one who stopped outside the café?"

"Mike." I can barely bring myself to say his name.

"Is he . . ." Cody pauses. "Is he okay?"

"Absolutely not."

"Yeah, I thought as much . . ." Cody looks at me. "He's the son of the guy who runs the campsite where I'm staying."

"You're at Country Life?" Damn. I don't like the thought of Cody being around Mike.

Cody nods. "I'm sleeping in a little dome tent."

I'm already picturing him in one of those tiny tents you can barely fit a single mat into. Somehow it totally fits with the image I have of him.

"Are you scared of him?" asks Cody.

I nod. There's no point denying it. My whole body goes on alert when I see Mike.

"Too bad," says Cody. "That you give him that power."

"What am I supposed to do?"

"Overcome your fear." Cody looks at me. "Next time don't walk away from him. Walk toward him. That's the quickest way to get over it."

If Cody thinks I'm ever going to get into Mike's convertible again voluntarily, he's got it wrong. I'd rather just be scared forever.

"Have you . . . have you ever spoken to Mike?" I ask cautiously.

Does he know what you're like? Maybe I should warn him about what you do to guys.

"No, I haven't," says Cody, and I sigh with relief. "But he seems kind of like a snake. Acting all friendly, but meanwhile . . . Those guys are the worst."

"You sound like you're speaking from experience."

"I am." Cody's face clouds over.

"Your dad?" I guess. This time I want to find out what's going on. Cody can't keep avoiding the subject while I bare my soul every time.

"*Ding, ding, ding!* You're going for the big prize." Cody smiles, but he looks sad.

"What . . ." I begin.

"Let's just say that my dad is a lot like your brother."

Cody pulls up his shirt, and I see a big blue bruise above his belt.

I gasp. "Did he . . . ?"

"Because I said I wanted to go on a road trip. So I went any-way. Obviously."

"Yeah . . ." I stare at the spot, now covered again by his shirt. "Did you speak to your dad again?"

"Not going to happen." Cody stares straight ahead. "I mur-dered him before I left."

I burst out laughing, but Cody doesn't join in.

Why would he say something like that?

I get that he hates his dad like I hate my brother, but he's not serious, is he?

It's too bad that the unbeatable feeling always fades away so quickly. And then you have to chase the thrill again.

My phone buzzes. It's my mom. I ignore it.

"What's up?" Cody nods at my phone. "Why don't you an-swer when your mom calls you?"

"Because she's only going to yell at me again."

"Maybe not. Maybe she just wants to say sorry."

"My mom?" I laugh. "Don't think so."

My phone buzzes again.

"Seems like she really wants to talk to you."

"She wants me to go to the beach with them like one big, happy family. Which we're not."

"Can't you just go lie on the sand and ignore the rest?" Cody makes it sound so easy.

I look at him. "Want to come along?"

Why did I ask him that? I barely know the guy.

"Yeah, cool," says Cody. "Sounds like fun."

I kind of regret the invitation, but at the same time, a warm feeling spreads through my body.

"You sure?" I look at him skeptically. "Spending the whole afternoon with my mom and dad and my scary brother?"

"Then I can keep an eye on him. If he gets aggressive, I can personally throw his ass into the sea."

I burst out laughing—and this time Cody does too.

Cody . . . He's your new plaything, right?

Then I call my mom back.

"Mom? Yeah, I'll come with you. But I want to bring someone along."

MARIA & HER MOM AND DAD

"He's a nice kid, that Cody." My dad is lying on a towel, wearing that bucket hat that always makes me cringe.

My mom is looking over at the beach bar, where Cody went to buy ice cream. He's been gone a long time.

"Why didn't you ask Pip to come along?"

"It's over."

Ferris glances at me. He barely said anything in the car, but he stared at Cody a few times.

"Over?" Mom looks at me in surprise. "You never mentioned it."

"No, I didn't."

"And you and Cody?"

"He's just a friend."

We both know you can't make regular friends.

"Well, he seems considerate." My mom picks up her magazine. "I agree with your father."

I remember what Cody said about his dad. *I murdered him before I left.*

Why would he say something like that?

My phone buzzes, and when I look, I see "MG" appear on the screen.

MARIA & MYSTERY GUEST

MYSTERY GUEST:

What do they have in store for me this time?

They don't say a word about the photo, but they know they have me completely in their power.

That photo must *never* get out. I'd do anything to prevent that. Anything.

MARIA:

MYSTERY GUEST:

MARIA:

I'm not going to make it.
I'm still on the beach.

MYSTERY GUEST:

I can see that.

Startled, I glance around. MG is *here*?!

The beach is packed with tourists of all shapes and sizes. A mom and dad with little kids are sitting nearby, making a sandcastle.

Behind us is a couple in love, who can hardly keep their hands off each other.

There's an older guy burning himself on a pale-blue beach towel.

Mystery Guest is bluffing.

They're not here.

But the last time I thought they were just trying to upset me, they sent that photo. Maybe I should start taking them a bit more seriously.

They say what they'll do, and they do what they say.

Cody finally comes back from the beach bar. He's carrying five ice creams, which are already starting to melt.

"Nice," says my dad. "Thanks, man."

"You're welcome," Cody smiles. I don't know what kind of instruction manual he's read, but my parents seem to like him.

If only I'd had that instruction manual for Pip's dad.

Pip.

Don't think about her.

I take my ice cream and quickly lick the drips off the cone.

"Aren't you feeling hot?" my dad asks Cody. "In those jeans?"

"A bit, but luckily there are a few air holes in them."

My dad bursts out laughing.

The rest of their conversation passes me by, because I suddenly realize that Cody had plenty of time to send me those messages.

He was inside that beach bar for ages.

What if he . . . ?

No, he couldn't have. He doesn't have a phone. He told me that himself.

But what if he lied? I look at his jeans, full of holes. What if there's a phone in one of those pockets?

A feeling of vulnerability washes over me again: I might just be sitting on the same towel as the culprit . . .

It's too bad that the unbeatable feeling always fades away so quickly. And then you have to chase the thrill again.

What if I'm his new thrill?

Threatening me and seeing how far I'll go with his dangerous challenges?

I think about when I used to steal money from Mom's wallet. Maybe Cody enjoys secrets as much as I do.

But how would he have gotten the photo he sent me last night?

He's never been to this town before, has he?

I study Cody again. His beautiful, tanned skin, his dark eyes, his sweet smile with that one crooked tooth . . . And the way he appeared out of nowhere and helped me when I was coming back from the lookout tower in a complete panic.

Isn't he simply too good to be true?

Maybe there's only one way to find out . . .

"Cody?"

Cody looks up. "What is it?"

"How about we take a walk?"

MARIA & CODY

"Delicious," says Cody as he puts the last bit of his cone into his mouth. "Coconut's my favorite. How was your lemon?"

"Good." I look at our feet as we walk through the surf. My red nail polish is wearing off. I need to touch it up.

"Your brother is calmer than I expected," says Cody.

"Ferris is holding back because you're here," I say.

"You think?"

"I know."

"Am I that scary?"

"I think you've made an impression on him." I turn to look at him. "And if you ask me, my dad's fallen in love with you."

Cody bursts out laughing. "I'm good with parents."

"Have you had a lot of girlfriends?"

"A few."

"A few?"

"Okay, a lot."

That answer doesn't surprise me at all.

I glance down at his hands, which he puts in his pockets. How am I going to find out if there's a phone in there?

"How about taking a selfie? The two of us together?" I suggest. "We'll have to do it with yours. Mine's back where we were sitting."

"I don't have a phone. Remember?" says Cody, and then he looks at me. "Hey, did you hear from that Mystery Guest person again?"

He asks it so casually that I suddenly can't believe I thought he had anything to do with it.

I actually feel a little ashamed.

"You told me about them yourself. Remember?" says Cody when I don't react immediately.

"I know," I say. "They . . . they just sent me a location."

Again, that neutral look.

"Are you going there?"

I have no choice.

"I think so."

"Want me to come with you?"

"You mean it?"

"Why not? A bit of adventure might be fun."

Cody kicks at a puddle of seawater, splashing my pants. "Let's go."

MARIA:

Why are you spying on me?

The path off the beach is so hot. I hear Cody panting behind me. I can barely make it up the slope myself.

My mom and dad and Ferris are staying at the beach a bit longer, so we'll have to take the bus. It only comes by twice an hour, and when we get to the bus stop, we see that we've just missed one.

"Damn!" Cody hits the glass wall of the bus shelter. "Damn, damn, damn!"

"What's wrong?"

"I hate waiting." Cody walks up and down in front of the bus stop, sweat on his forehead.

"I thought you were the relaxed type?"

Cody nods. "Ninety percent of the time."

"And the other ten percent?"

"That's apparently when I'm with you. Whoa, it's so hot today . . ."

I nod. There's hardly any shade at the bus stop. It's like sitting in a glass sauna.

Cody waits at the edge of the sidewalk, leaning against the glass of the bus shelter.

Some girls on bikes go past, looking at Cody. I recognize them from school. They're a year younger. When Cody waves at them, they giggle.

"Everyone seems to be in love with you," I say.

"How about you?" Cody says, looking at me over his shoulder.

He's your new plaything, right?

That's what Pip said less than twenty-four hours ago, and now I'm seriously wondering about the answer to that question.

"No," I say quickly.

Then the girls come back. They brake right in front of the bus stop, cool as you like, and speak to Cody. "Hey, we wanted to ask you . . . Can we get your number? There's a party tonight at Outcast and . . ."

"I don't have a phone," says Cody.

"Oh . . ." One of the girls blushes. She probably thinks he's rejecting them outright.

"Hey, but I might come," says Cody. "So maybe I'll see you guys this evening."

"Yeah . . ." The girl smiles. "See you tonight, then."

When they've gone, I shake my head. "You broke their hearts."

"Sometimes you have to," says Cody. "Harsh but true." He looks at me. "You have a girlfriend, right?"

"Had," I correct him.

"Huh? Is it over?"

"Yeah. Since yesterday."

"What went wrong?"

"Her ex threatened me."

Cody frowns. "There are a lot of sick people living around here!"

I burst out laughing. "You can say that again."

"So you broke up with her because her ex wanted you to? That can't be the only reason, can it?" Cody pauses. "My last girlfriend seemed perfect, but we weren't a good match. I wanted to do more than just sit together on the couch. I wanted to go out, to do things together." He sighs. "I felt like we both had to change too much so that we could like each other. Then you know it's not working."

I look up. "Sounds familiar. Pip is really chill. I'm not. She wants peace and quiet. I want . . ."

"Action." Something flickers in Cody's eyes. "Now, that's something that I recognize."

"Life can be so *boring*."

"Was she boring too?"

"Yeah." Before I know it, I've blurted it out. The word just slips out of my mouth.

Cody grins. "Ouch. Well, that's certainly honest."

"Yes, sorry. Pip *was* boring," I say quietly. "But she couldn't help it. That's who she is."

"But not you."

I glance at Cody. It's like I drew the perfect person, and he came to life right in front of me.

"No," I reply. "Boring—that's not me."

Then a red convertible pulls up next to the bus stop.

"Need a ride?" Mike shouts.

"No," I reply immediately.

"It's going to be at least twenty minutes before the bus arrives, and it has to be sweltering in that shelter. Come on. Get in."

Then he looks at Cody. "You too."

Cody turns to look at me. His eyes are sparkling.

I know what he's going to say, but I'm not doing it. No way.

Then Cody leans in and whispers the words against my skin. "Overcome your fear, Maria. Together, with me."

Those last three words have a strange effect on me. It's as if I'm being lifted. As if I'm floating above the ground.

"Don't let him win." Then Cody opens the passenger door and points at the back seat. "You going there? Then I'll go in the front."

The back seat, which is etched in my memory.

I have to overcome my fear, or Mike will go on winning every time.

"Okay," I say, getting in. I avoid Mike's gaze. "One ride. And that's all."

"So, what do you think of Maria, Cody?"

Suddenly I understand why Mike offered us the ride. He intends to make life very difficult for me . . .

Cody's plan for getting me to overcome my fear suddenly feels incredibly dumb.

I'll always be afraid of Mike, no matter how many times I see him. The way he shouted Shannon's name across the fields . . .

The guy is seriously disturbed.

"We have fun together," says Cody.

"Just a bit of fun? Or *really* good fun? If that's the case, you'd better watch out, because . . ." Mike glances at me in the rearview mirror. "Maria eats boys alive. And girls too. The way she dumped poor little Pippi!"

I can't be bothered to correct him again. Cody just looks straight at the road ahead and doesn't respond.

If he has an opinion on this bizarre conversation, he's good at hiding it.

When we finally reach our destination, I notice that Mike has stopped right next to the location of the dropped pin.

Is it a coincidence? Or did Mike know exactly where we should be because he was the one who sent the location?

I look at him. I didn't see him as Mystery Guest at all, but he might still surprise me.

After all, I didn't expect him to ever return to town either.

Cody opens the door and jumps like he can't wait to get out of the car.

"Good luck with her, Cody," Mike shouts after him. "That's a free tip from me to you."

What is Mike up to? How come he's so confident when he knows the whole town hates him? Why did he come back this summer? Just to help his dad with the campsite? Or because he wanted to scare the hell out of me with this MG stuff?

I watch the red car as it disappears into the distance.

Cody snatches an envelope from a traffic sign at the bottom of the grassy slope that leads up to the highway.

"Hey," I shout. "That's for me."

"Better read it quickly, then." Cody hands me the envelope.

I take out the card, my eyes darting along the lines. The words feel like blows.

"No . . ." I hear Cody say as he reads the card over my shoulder. "This is really bad . . ."

MARIA & MYSTERY GUEST

"Cross the highway?" Cody's voice falters. "They can't be serious, can they?"

I know how busy the highway is; it's the connection between our town and the big city. Thousands of cars drive along it every day.

Then I read the rest.

"What are they talking about?"

But Cody is already gone. He's striding up the grass slope.

I don't hesitate for a second. I go after him. What the hell has MG put up there?

At the top of the slope, dozens of cars go racing past.

Small cars, camper vans, trucks . . .

It takes me a moment to see through the wall of vehicles, but then I catch a glimpse of the median strip.

There's a small space between the two guardrails, and in that space there's a pet carrier.

Inside the carrier I see a ginger cat, looking completely lost and helpless.

My heart skips a beat.

"Jax . . ."

MARIA & CODY

It's Pip's cat.

"Jax!" Like he can hear me through all that traffic. And there's no way I'll be able to calm him down from this distance.

How long has the poor little guy been there? Ever since I received the location?

Mystery Guest said I had to be here within the hour, but I took my sweet time and went for a stroll along the beach with Cody first.

Jax must have been here at least an hour and a half!

Without stopping to think, I swing my leg over the guardrail.

I have to get him away from there as quickly as possible.

Cody's even faster than me. He's already over the rail, and I quickly switch on my camera.

Got to make sure I get a video this time.

A horn blares, and I see the driver tapping his forehead. Crazy. A millisecond, and then he's gone.

"Now!" Cody starts running.

No time for doubt. I run after him. Car horns honk, and a blue van screeches past, right in front of us.

I freeze, standing there between the lanes of traffic. I can't run on; there are three more cars coming. And there's a truck approaching on the lane behind me.

"We're alive, Maria!" Cody grabs my hand and gives it a squeeze. "Breathe!"

Even now he has a big grin on his face, as if he's untouchable.

I feel the adrenaline rushing through my body.

We're alive.

The truck races past behind us. The gust of air almost sucks me under, but Cody holds my hand even tighter.

We're alive.

And then finally we can run the last few steps to the other side.

I dive onto the ground to grab the pet carrier. Jax barely reacts when I stick my finger through the bars. I feel his warm body panting away.

"He needs water," I yell. "Now!"

What kind of sicko leaves a cat out in direct sunlight for hours?

"I have some in my bag," shouts Cody. He takes the carrier from me and runs back across the road in one go.

To my surprise, he reaches the other side in a few easy steps, but I hesitate longer, and another wave of cars and a truck comes racing along.

The same thing happens as up on the lookout tower. All my senses kick in at once: The asphalt vibrates, exhaust fumes fill my nostrils, the air shimmers.

"I can do this," I whisper. "We're alive!"

And then I run. A small yellow car swerves to avoid me, and I hear loud honking, squealing tires, and someone yelling.

Then it's quiet.

I'm still alive.

And the car has driven off.

I made it!

With trembling legs, I join Cody at the bottom of the slope. He's crouching over the pet carrier and holding out water for Jax in a plastic bottle cap.

"Is he . . ." My breath catches in my throat, because I barely dare to ask the question. "Is he . . . okay?"

What if the shock and stress were too much for him? Pip will be heartbroken. And I'm sure she'll hate me forever.

"Come on," I hear Cody whisper. "You can do it, little guy."

"Cody! Answer me!"

Cody looks up. His eyes are serious. I'm not used to seeing that expression on his face. For a moment, he seems nothing at all like himself.

"He's drinking," says Cody.

"Yes!" I put my arms around him. Cody is about to return my hug, but he loses his balance. We fall backward onto the grass.

"You helped me!" I look at Cody. "I can't believe you crossed that highway."

Cody runs his eyes over my whole face, stopping at my lips. "It was time to take action, right?"

Then I press my lips to his. I know it's been less than twenty-four hours since I broke up with Pip, but still I kiss him like I've never kissed anyone before.

He's your new plaything, right?

I push away the thought of Pip, because the two of us were never meant to be.

Cody was right: Sometimes you have to change too much so that you can like someone else.

I don't have to do that with him. With Cody I can just be my craziest self, and he loves it because he's the same. Or even crazier.

I murdered him before I left.

Whether it's true or not, it doesn't matter anymore. If his dad was anything like Ferris, he deserved it.

I should have killed Ferris too.

I thought I'd outsmarted him, but it turned out he was a better manipulator than me. He convinced his counselors that he changed.

He's coming back to live at home.

Right now Cody is the only good thing in my life, so I'm kissing him.

Cody runs his hands over my back. He feels so much stronger than Pip ever did. When she did that, it was more like gentle stroking. Cody claws into me as if I'm his prey.

We roll to one side. Cody laughs between kisses.

Something falls into the grass.

"Oops . . ." Cody makes a grab for it.

"What is that?" I hear myself ask.

"Nothing." Cody quickly shoves it back into his pocket. It feels like I got hit by a car anyway—because I just about manage to see what it is.

I don't have a phone. Don't you know how harmful the radiation is?

It's a cell phone.

PIP

Of course she didn't see it coming, what I was going to do to her.

As far as she was concerned, I was *safe*.

CODY

She was on her guard against me.

I don't think she *really* trusted me.

But I think she secretly enjoyed that.

NORAH

If Maria had to bet on her murderer?

Then she'd have put all her money on me.

MARIA & PIP

take three deep breaths, and then I ring the bell.

It doesn't take long—the door swings open, and I'm looking at Pip's face.

"Jax?!" Pip stares at the pet carrier with wide eyes. Then she looks at me, and her eyes narrow.

"What did you do to him?!"

"Nothing," I say quickly. "He . . ."

"Give him here!" Pip grabs Jax and slides her fingers through the bars of the pet carrier. "Are you okay?"

Jax seems to have perked up quite a bit. It was Cody's idea to get him a can of cat food in town.

I managed not to give anything away when I saw his phone, but I was glad when he said he couldn't come to the pet store with me because he had to get back to the campsite.

I wanted to be alone so I could think.

Why did Cody lie about his phone? So I wouldn't see him

as a suspect? Or was he just trying to keep up his hippie act? The free spirit in his tent without a phone . . .

After going to the pet store, I sat for an hour with Jax in the shade of a big tree before I finally dared to go to Pip's.

Jax is meowing away, and Pip keeps giving him little kisses through the door.

I'm about to turn and leave, but Pip stops me.

"Hang on a moment. He's been missing for hours! He never goes outside normally. You know he's always in my bedroom. So where did you find him?"

"You seriously do not want to know," I say quietly.

Pip hesitates. I know she'd prefer to send me away, but at the same time, she wants to hear what I have to say.

She holds the door open.

"Come on in."

Pip puts the pet carrier on the kitchen counter and opens the door. Jax warily steps out, as if he's afraid that a car might still come racing past at any moment.

"Tell me," says Pip. "Where *was* Jax?"

"On the highway," I say reluctantly.

"What?!"

"He was in the middle of the highway," I say. "Mystery Guest left him there."

"What?!" Pip's voice is getting louder and louder. "You're still playing that game with that sicko?!"

I have no choice.

"Yes."

"Damn it, Maria . . ." It's the first time I've ever heard Pip curse. "I warned you about that creep!"

"I know."

Pip's face clouds over. Then she asks quietly, "What . . . what kinds of things do they make you do?"

"All sorts." I don't want to talk about this with her.

"How did you get Jax off the highway?"

"By running really fast."

Pip strokes Jax's fur and shakes her head, as if she still can't quite believe what I'm telling her.

"Were you alone?"

I can hear the question she's not asking. Pip obviously wants to know if Cody was with me.

"Yes," I say. I watch her face closely, and she seems to believe my lie.

"So you risked your own life to save Jax?"

Pip's voice sounds less and less angry.

"Yes." I look at the cat. "You know how cool I think Jax is."

"And what about me?" Pip glances at me, but her gaze moves on. "Do you miss me?"

"Yes."

In a way, it's true. I miss her gentle kisses on my shoulder.

But I also need someone like Cody, who kisses me wildly. What I'd really like is to have both of them.

I know that's impossible, that it's an incredibly selfish thought, but that's how it is.

Pip and Cody would be the perfect combination for me . . .

"Want some cake? My mom baked it this morning."

I look up with a grateful smile. "Nice."

I check my phone, but there's still no answer from Mystery Guest, not to the most recent messages I sent either.

> MARIA sent a video.
>
> MARIA:
>
> Here it is. Happy now?
>
> This is the life of an innocent animal.
>
> You are going way too far!
>
> Do you know something? Do whatever you want with that video. I quit.

Maybe I shouldn't have sent that message. The last thing I want to do is make them mad.

But I'm mad too. They should have kept their hands off Jax. They went too far . . .

"Here you go. Coconut cake. It's so good." Pip places a large piece of cake in front of me. It's a slice from the edge. I'm touched that she remembered that's my favorite bit.

Even now that I've broken up with her, she still keeps trying to please me.

Again, I feel guilty about that kiss with Cody.

What would she do if I told her, if I was honest?

"Norah came round," Pip says out of nowhere.

"What? Why?"

"She wanted to ask how I was doing. She was actually really sweet . . ."

Jealousy rears its head inside me like a monster.

"Of course she was sweet. She wants you back."

"That wasn't it. It was just a friendly visit."

"Norah can't just be friends."

"Then that's something you guys have in common," says Pip.

"I'm here, aren't I?" I say. "And we're not kissing. We're just talking to each other as friends."

Pip's face lights up a little. "Would you like to? Kiss, I mean?"

I think of Cody, of his full lips kissing me as if we might die at any moment. It was a kiss like I've never had before, full of life.

"The two of us are better as friends," I say, and Pip seems to shrink.

"I don't feel ready to kiss anyone else for now," I quickly add.

Pip wraps her fingers around her cup. I can see she's thinking about my reply. "Okay . . ."

134

"And what about you?" I ask, to shift the attention from myself. "Is there someone you'd like to kiss?"

Pip takes a sip of tea but doesn't reply.

"Well?" I press her. "Are you going back to Norah?"

"No way," says Pip, but I'm not convinced. For the first time since we met, I have the feeling that she's lying to me.

MARIA & HER MOM AND DAD

"There you are." My mom and dad and Ferris are sitting at the table when I go into the kitchen. "We were just about to eat."

I see the lasagna in the oven dish: Ferris's favorite.

"There's plenty to go around." Mom fills a plate. "Are you eating with us? Or did you have something with Cody?"

"No. That'd be nice."

"He's a cool guy," says my dad. "Got a real sense of humor."

And he's an amazing liar, I think.

I take a big mouthful. "It's so good," I say to my mom. It's way too hot, but I swallow it anyway.

"Thanks. It's the old recipe." Mom looks at Ferris, then me, and back again. She doesn't seem mad about this morning anymore, but I hope she's not going to get sentimental about all four of us sitting at the table together.

"Ferris would like to brighten up his old room a little," says Dad. "Want me to paint your room too?"

I look up. The fact that Ferris is coming back home hits me

again. I glance at him across the table, where he's shoveling down lasagna.

"I don't need a new color," I say.

"You sure? Isn't all that black a bit . . . gloomy?"

"What do you mean?"

"It's kind of like a coffin," says my dad.

Ferris bursts out laughing.

"I find it restful" is all I say.

"Rest in peace," says Ferris. "Sounds about right."

"Shut your mouth," I snarl at him.

"Hey." Mom shakes her head. "I don't want to hear that kind of talk at the table."

I bite the inside of my cheek.

Ferris pushes his plate away. "I'm going over to Joe's."

"Okay," Mom says.

Ferris is about to leave, but then he comes back and takes his plate to the sink.

"Thanks," he says to Mom, and gives her a kiss. He looks pointedly at me as if he wants to say, *This is how to do it. This is how you fool her.*

"It's going to be a late one, I think."

"Say hi to Joe," says Dad. "And no . . ."

He falls silent.

"And no *what*?" Ferris looks at him.

"Don't drink too much," says Dad, but he kind of blushes.

"And no *drugs*," says Ferris. "That's what you wanted to say, isn't it?"

Dad takes a bite of his lasagna. His cheeks are now the same color as the sauce.

"I don't do drugs anymore," says Ferris. "I'm not addicted or something."

"Your dad's just worried," Mom says, trying to calm him down. "Don't take it the wrong way."

"He's calling me a junkie."

"That's not true," says Mom.

I poke the cheesy crust of my lasagna, not knowing where to look. It's like the temperature in the kitchen just went down a few degrees.

"When I'm finished at the center for good, you guys need to give me a chance." Ferris is staring at my dad, who's avoiding his gaze. "Or I'm going to go live somewhere else."

"You are coming here," says Mom. "We're so happy you're coming home."

"You too?" Ferris speaks directly to Dad. "Or would you rather your junkie son stayed away?"

"Oh, that's not . . ." begins Mom, but Ferris slams his fist on the table.

"I was asking *him*!"

The ticking of the clock is the only sound in the kitchen.

How can my mom and dad think he's changed? Ferris is a ticking time bomb. The question isn't whether he'll explode but *when*.

"Sorry." Ferris rubs his scalp. The rasping sound is as unbearable as nails on a blackboard. "I got carried away for a moment there. But it makes me so mad when you guys don't trust me."

Dad finally looks up. "Of course we trust you, son. Sorry about what I said."

He's lying.

But it doesn't matter. Ferris has him exactly where he wants him.

MARIA & MYSTERY GUEST

Why has MG stopped responding?

It's making me so nervous. I have no idea if they're mad or not.

I'm lying on my bed, clicking on the conversation over and over again, as if that might change something.

But MG is as silent as the grave.

I can hear my mom and dad talking downstairs, but I can't make out what they're saying.

Bet it's about Ferris.

After he left, it was silent in the kitchen. For the rest of the meal, no one said a word.

Mom loaded the dishwasher. Dad went out to mow the lawn.

As I stare up at my bedroom ceiling, my phone vibrates. Mystery Guest has finally resurfaced.

MYSTERY GUEST:

I did what I wanted with the photo.
Like you said.

I sit up. What did they do?

MARIA:

What?

MYSTERY GUEST:

There's a party at Outcast tonight.

Go there and find out.

MARIA & OUTCAST

The bass makes my body vibrate.

It seems like all the kids from the surrounding area have come to Outcast tonight. I've never seen it this busy before. Loads of people are standing around the bar, a converted shipping container, waiting to buy a drink.

There are people dancing everywhere, out in the open air. Everyone calls Outcast a nightclub, but it's just a few speakers under the starry sky.

The shaded seating areas with beanbags create a cozy atmosphere.

I can see lots of people from my school, but there's no trace of MG.

I'm surprised to see Ferris standing at the bar with Mike.

He said he was going to Joe's, didn't he? But Joe is nowhere to be seen. Instead, Ferris is chatting away with the local drug dealer.

When did those two start talking to each other?

I thought Mike just sold him drugs that night, but now they seem to be chatting almost like buddies.

Two outcasts.

I really don't like the thought of the two of them talking.

What could they be discussing? Me? I sneak a bit closer, staying in the shadow of the trees.

As the music changes, a loud cheer goes up.

If I want to find out what they're saying, I'm going to have to get closer. But how am I going to do that without them seeing me?

Ferris suddenly looks up, and I quickly duck behind one of the trees.

Did he see me?

My heart pounding, I lean against the tree. When I cautiously peep around the trunk, I see that they're gone.

Huh? Where did they go?

"Well, well. Who do we have here?" says a voice in my ear.

My body freezes. I don't even need to turn around to see who it is. Her voice has the effect of an ice-cold bath on me.

"How's single life agreeing with you?"

MARIA & NORAH

N orah.

How does she always manage to sneak up on me from behind? That's the second time this week!

"It's going great," I reply. Where did Mike and Ferris go? Did they see me?

"I have to talk to you about Pip," says Norah.

"There's no need now," I say, scanning the site.

"You don't get to decide that."

"I broke up with her." I turn and look into her white doll-like face. "So you and I are done."

I turn back to the bar. If I see them, I'll go after them. Mike and Ferris are not a good combination. It can't end well . . .

But then I feel something around my throat. Before I can react, my head is roughly pulled back.

My hands shoot to my neck, but I'm completely defenseless. I feel a coarse rope cutting into my skin.

"What . . ." My voice disappears into a mass of gurgling.

Norah! She's strangling me!

"Shh." Norah's mouth is close to my ear. She smells so strongly of vanilla that it makes me dizzy. "You are going to shut your mouth and listen. Got it?"

I can barely even nod.

"I was at Pip's today. She told me about your breakup, but something wasn't right."

My vision starts to blur. Feels like I'm running out of air.

"She didn't seem at all sad when I asked about you. Don't you think that's strange?"

What is Norah talking about? She has to let go of me. Now.

"How is that possible?" Norah hisses the words in my ear. "Well?"

"Maybe . . ." I gasp. Norah has to loosen the rope a little to hear the rest of my sentence. "Maybe . . . she was faking it?"

"She wasn't." Norah pulls it tighter again.

My phone buzzes in my pocket. If I can grab it, I can call someone. I squeeze one hand into my pocket, still trying to loosen the rope with the other.

I can feel the top of my phone now, but I'm getting dizzier and dizzier.

I think I'm about to collapse.

"N-Noraaaaah . . ." My voice fails me.

"I know Pip," she continues, as cool as anything. "I know the look on her face when she's in love."

In love?

What is Norah talking about?

Suddenly she lets go of me, and I fall onto the soft ground, gasping for breath. My throat feels like a thousand needles are sticking into it. It's much worse than when I swallowed MG's drink.

Breathing hurts so much, but I force myself to take another gulp of oxygen. And another, and another . . .

"And she's not in love with you or with me," Norah adds.

Norah's words slowly get through to me.

Has Pip met someone else?

But when could that have happened?

While I was at the beach with Cody?

Does Pip want to get back at me for breaking up with her? That's not her style at all.

"That . . ." I try to speak, but my voice sounds like the rope is still around my neck. "That's . . . not . . . possible."

"Apparently it is." Norah spits on the ground, right next to my feet. "So do something about it."

MARIA & MYSTERY GUEST

Norah is gone. Still panting, I take my phone from my pocket.

The message that just arrived is from MG.

I look at the dark woods behind me, where Norah just disappeared. She couldn't have sent this, because she was still holding on to me when the message came in.

Wasn't she?

I take a raspy breath. How long is this pain going to last? When I look into my selfie camera, I gasp.

There are fiery red welts running across my neck. I'm going to have to wear a scarf for the next few days, or people are going to notice.

When I touch my neck, the pain makes me flinch.

Why did Norah do that? Because she wanted to show me that she's still in charge?

She's disturbed enough to be Mystery Guest.

But what about Jax?

Would she really leave Pip's cat on the highway?

She loves that animal. Pip told me so herself.

And how could she have sent me this last message? Did she do it when she let go of me for a moment so that I could speak? Did she quickly press send?

MARIA:

Why did I have to come here? I don't see anything.

MYSTERY GUEST:

Check across the way.

Across the way?

Do they know where I am right now?

Are they watching me from a distance again?

I look over at the bar, which is pretty quiet. Still no sign of Mike and Ferris.

On the wall there are posters saying *Endless Summer*—that's tonight's theme. With photos of beaches, sunsets, palm trees, and

My breath catches in my throat.

On one of the posters, I see a grainy version of myself.

It's the photo of that night by the church.

You can't recognize me immediately, but if you take a closer look, you can tell it's me.

My brown curls are clearly visible, as is my sharp nose.

And I have a blue jerry can in my hands.

MARIA & PIP

I stand in front of the poster, and behind my back, I tug it off the wall in one movement.

Did anyone see?

All around me, people go on dancing. No one is paying any attention to me.

I look at the picture in my hand. Mystery Guest wanted me to find the poster, but why?

If they wanted to expose me, they wouldn't have told me about it, would they? They'd have just left the poster hanging there until everyone at the party had seen it.

"Maria?"

Startled, I look up and find myself face to face with Pip.

Where did she suddenly come from?

"Pip . . ." I crumple the poster and stuff it into my back pocket.

"What are those marks on your neck?" Pip says, pointing. The poster almost made me forget Norah's attempt to strangle me.

"I . . ." I shake my head. "What are you doing here?"

"Partying," says Pip. "Like everyone else."

"But . . . but you don't do parties."

Pip's face clouds over, as if I just insulted her. "Yeah, I do."

She looks around, and then her face brightens up.

"Ah, there she is. Catch you later, Maria."

She?

I see Pip heading toward a girl with short bleached hair. Pip gives her a kiss on the cheek.

It feels like being struck by lightning.

Who *is* she?

Pip laughs at something the girl says and even puts a hand on her knee. The two of them are sitting together on the beanbags, the spot where it all started for Pip and me.

Do something about it.

The last thing I want to do is follow more commands from Norah, but this time it was the best order she could have given.

There's nothing I would like more than to do something about this.

Within seconds I'm standing beside them, holding out my hand to the girl.

"Hey, I'm Maria."

"Er . . ." The girl shakes my hand doubtfully. "Pomme."

I burst out laughing. "As in the French word for 'apple'?"

The girl shakes her head and sighs, as if I'm her little sister who thinks she's a comedian.

"Mind if I sit with you guys?" Before either can answer, I drop down onto a third beanbag.

"I'm . . . a friend of Pip's," I add. "And who might you be?"

"Her date."

My blood goes from boiling to freezing. Norah was right.

"How do you know each other?"

"Maria . . ." Pip's voice sounds pleading. "Would you please leave us alone for a while?"

"Why?"

"Because . . ." Pip turns a little red.

"Because you want to kiss her, right?" I look directly at Pip, but as always, she avoids my gaze. "I thought you weren't ready for that yet?"

At the other end of the bar, some guys start whooping. They down shots and jump up and down.

"And who exactly are you?" Pomme looks at me with a frown.

"Her girlfriend," I say.

"Ex," Pip corrects me. "You broke up with me."

"And now I'm starting it up again," I say. Turning to Pomme, I add, "So you can leave."

"Maria!" Pip's cheeks are bright red. "Just stop it!"

"I don't know what's going on here, but . . ." Pomme slowly stands up.

"No, stay." Pip tries to pull her back, but Pomme is already walking away.

"What are you *doing*?" Pip yells.

"What am *I* doing?" I can't believe Pip seriously just said that. "Since when did you start dating other people? She's not even your type. You like brunettes; she's super blond. And a nose piercing? Really?"

"How do you know what my type is?" Pip snarls.

"I know you."

"Believe me: You don't." Pip's eyes are shooting fire. For the first time since I've known her, she's looking straight at me.

And not just a glance, but a stare that lasts for seconds.

"Pip," I say quietly. "Come on . . ."

She's going to come around now, just like she finally came around after ignoring me for two days.

We'll sit on the beanbags together all night, like we did in December. Both of us drinking a few too many drinks, so *everything* is amusing.

It was one of the few times I ever saw Pip buzzed. I always thought she'd never let herself go like that.

It might be my favorite night we spent together.

"Pip?"

Pip is still looking at me when she says, "Go away, Maria."

"But . . . you don't mean that. I . . ."

"I'm going to find Pomme." Pip stands up, and without looking at me again, she walks away.

Pip does not come back.

I wait for ages, but Pip is *really* gone. As I walk to my bike, I see that Mystery Guest has sent me another message.

I don't want to know what they have to say.

I've lost Pip.

For good this time.

Instead of opening the message, I put my phone back in my pocket.

And that's when I see them.

Pomme is leaning against the wall of the container. Pip is leaning against her.

It's like a scene from a movie, one I'd rather not watch.

The kind of movie you know will haunt your nightmares forever.

Pip is clawing her hands in Pomme's hair as if she's her prey.

She's kissing Pomme the way Cody kissed *me*, like her life depends on it.

Do something about it.

But now there's nothing that can be done.

MARIA & SHANNON

The flashlight on my phone is barely bright enough. I can see the fence I parked in front of with Mike, but there's no sign of the cows.

They're fast asleep, of course, safe and sound in their shed.

Why don't I just go home myself?

Why would I come here, in the middle of the night?

"Is this where you were lying, Shannon? Or was it over there?"

I'm startled by how loud my voice sounds in the darkness.

What am I doing? Why am I talking to someone who's long dead?

"Can I ask you what it felt like to die? Did it hurt? Maybe being dead isn't such a bad thing . . ."

My words hang in the air. I'm ashamed of what I said. I'm sure Shannon would have wanted to live for longer.

"Sorry," I say. "But sometimes I just want *everything* to stop."

I clasp my hands around the bars of the fence.

"You're a celebrity, Shannon. Everyone knows your name.

The whole town was talking about you, and so was everyone else for miles around. I don't know if that would happen if I died. If anyone would miss me at all. Mom only thinks about Ferris, and even Dad keeps standing up for him these days. They can see he's still the same old Ferris, but they're letting him come home anyway. Mike is back, and he seems to be up to something. And Pip . . ."

My voice falters for a moment.

"Pip's found a replacement for me."

Why am I telling Shannon all of this? As if she can hear me!

But maybe it's good no one can hear me. Maybe this is the only way to tell the story.

"What will Mom and Dad do when they hear the truth? When they hear about what I did that night . . . That it was me who . . . They'll have me locked up! Mom will never trust me again. Dad will take her side. And Ferris? Yeah, he'll think it's hilarious. This cannot get out. You understand? Never."

In the distance, I hear the beat pumping at Outcast. Are Pip and Pomme still kissing?

"Ferris had to go," I say. "He was dangerous. Do you know how I got this scar?"

I point at a mark above my eyebrow.

"We were playing a board game when I was about nine. I was winning, and I started teasing Ferris. So he swept the game straight off the table. When I yelled at him that he should behave himself, he threw his cup of tea at me. It hit me on the forehead, and I had a huge cut. And do you know what

156

my mom said when we had to go to the emergency room for stitches? That I knew better than to confront him like that."

I wipe my eyes, but the tears soon come back.

"She said I knew what he was like and that I should be a bit more careful around him. The way she spoke to me, it was like it was *my* fault that he couldn't control himself."

I'm squeezing the fence so hard now that it hurts.

"So Ferris had to go, as far away as possible. And that night in December, he was completely out of it. I think Mike's drugs hit him the wrong way. After I dropped Pip off at home, I went back to the party. But just before, I took a wrong turn. I didn't go back to Outcast. I had to go through with my plan. My insane, dangerous, totally wild plan."

I pause for breath.

"It was like, all at once, I completely sobered up from all those drinks Pip and I had had that night. The plan was perfectly thought-out. Ferris was going to go past on his way back home. All I had to do was make sure the fire was blazing. And what burns better than gas? Ferris always has a jerry can in our shed, for his scooter."

I can picture it now. I'd already hidden the jerry can there that afternoon, under a pile of branches.

"The fire spread so easily," I say quietly. "There was a huge sea of flames. It was a magical sight."

Why am I telling her this?

There's no way Shannon's going to tell anyone else, but I don't like the idea of my words hanging above the fields.

But still, I go on talking. It's as if my mouth is relieved that the truth is finally coming out.

"But the flames just spread and spread, and I got scared, so I ran off. I was home before Ferris. He got back half an hour after me. And in that time, I was able to tell Mom and Dad what I'd seen. Ferris starting a fire. They didn't believe me. Of course they didn't. Until he got home, completely out of it. Mom was horrified. Ferris couldn't walk in a straight line, and he was shouting all kinds of weird stuff. He punched Dad. Right in the face. Right here."

That was the moment when I knew I was going to win. As long as I stuck to my story.

Ferris started the fire.

He wouldn't remember a thing about it because of the drugs.

No one would doubt it because Ferris had already been labeled as a boy who was out of control.

That's what the school management said. That's what my mom and dad knew.

During the court case, my story came across as clear and credible.

And Ferris?

He freaked out in the courtroom.

Then I was *certain* it was all over for him, because the judge could see what he was really like.

Ferris was going away to the center, and I was rid of him.

"Pip and I officially started dating," I say, ending the story. "It was like my life was finally going in the right direction."

I see Pip and Pomme in front of me again.

"Pip was always there, *always*. How could she . . ."

Then my phone buzzes, and I see that it's Pip.

PIP:

Pomme is a better kisser than you.

I stare at the message, but I can't believe what it says. How could she send that?

Pip doesn't do that kind of thing. She's way too nice.

I want to reply, but I have no idea what to say.

I'm about to put my phone back in my pocket when my eye falls on the unread message from Mystery Guest, and I go ahead and read their words.

MYSTERY GUEST:

That wasn't the only poster, btw.

There are another ten of them hanging around town. Good luck.

MARIA & CODY

Where are they?

Where did Mystery Guest put them?

I need to find those things before it gets light out and everyone sees them.

Maria with a blue jerry can in her hands. Maybe people won't realize what's going on at first sight, but if my mom and dad get to see that poster . . .

Then I see a poster on the window of the bakery.

That's number one!

As quickly as I can, I ride my bike over there and tear it into pieces.

Where are the rest? I have nine more to go!

MYSTERY GUEST:

Can you find them? :)

They're enjoying this . . .

Whoever it is, they want nothing more than to see me suffer.

I think about Norah, who has narrowly avoided killing me on two occasions.

What MG is doing—it's exactly the kind of thing she'd do . . .

I wheel around and see the next poster on a lamppost. The posters show just my photo, without any words.

That grainy photo, which is just sharp enough.

Mystery Guest was there that night.

While I thought I was alone, someone was secretly watching me from the bushes.

All those months, they kept this photograph, and I knew nothing about it.

Photograph . . .

I think of Cody and his camera. Could he be behind this after all?

But then why is he only coming out with it now?

Why is everything happening all at once?

Ferris coming home, Mike spending the summer here, Norah going crazy, Cody appearing out of nowhere, Pip pushing me away, Mystery Guest . . .

What's the connection? What am I missing?

Who is doing all of this to me?

I spot another poster, and another one.

Six more to go . . .

There! I pull the next poster out from under the windshield wiper of a parked car.

As someone approaches on a bike, I feel my body cramp up. I need to be quick. These posters need to go before anyone else comes along.

But then, to my surprise, I see that it's Cody.

"Maria." Cody looks at me with a smile. "What's going on? Are you doing some kind of advertising stunt?"

I glance down at the last poster I found and quickly hide it behind my back. "No. The opposite. They need to come down."

Why did I say that? The last thing I want to do is involve someone else.

"So what does the poster say?" asks Cody.

When I don't answer, he gets off his bike.

"Want me to help you?"

He can't be Mystery Guest if he's offering to help, can he? MG *wants* me to get found out.

"Well?" Cody looks at me. "Yes or no?"

I really don't want Cody to see the poster, but what's worse? If he's the only one who sees it? Or if the whole town sees it?

"Yes. Please," I say, pushing the thought of his secret phone to the back of my mind. "There are another five of them."

We have all the posters except one.

Maybe Mystery Guest made a mistake, and there are only nine of them.

Or maybe they're lying on purpose so that I'll be roaming around all night.

It's slowly starting to get light out. My mom and dad will be awake soon.

When they find out I'm not in bed, all hell is going to break loose.

"I need to go home," I say.

"You sure?" Cody says, looking at me. "We're still missing one."

"Yep, I'm certain."

"Okay." Cody hands me the last crumpled poster, and I toss it into the nearest trash can.

He must have looked at the photo, but luckily he hasn't asked me about it.

"Thanks for your help," I say.

"You're welcome."

Cody and I look at each other for a few seconds, and it's as if I can hear the air crackling as I lean toward him.

I want to feel his lips again, his strong arms, his . . . But then Cody turns his cheek toward me, so my lips land there.

No clawing hands on my back, no teeth biting my bottom lip. Just a peck on his cheek.

"Good night, Maria," he says, getting back on his bike. "Catch you later."

MYSTERY GUEST:

If I'm not mistaken, you're missing one poster.

Want to guess where it is?

I brake just outside our front door. How does MG know that?

Was he there in town just now? Or am I a complete idiot, and is Cody . . .

At that moment, the front door opens, and I'm looking into my mom's face.

At least, I *know* it's my mom, but she looks like someone else. I can't figure out the look in her eyes at all.

I'm about to ask her what's wrong, but then I see what she's holding.

"Maria . . ." My mom's voice doesn't get any further than my name.

In her hands, she has the last of the posters.

MARIA & HER MOM AND DAD

" **I** . . ." I stare at the poster in her hands. Did MG bring it here?

But why?

Until now they were just threats, and there was always something I could do to stop them. Why have they suddenly changed the rules of the game?

"Come inside." My dad appears in the doorway. "We need to talk to you."

To talk.

But will they listen to me?

I look at my mom and dad.

Ferris's mom and dad.

Not mine.

I'm no one's favorite, and after today I never will be.

Now that they know the truth, they'll write me off for good. They won't arrange some expensive private clinic for me. They'll send me straight to prison.

I turn and jump back onto my bike.

"Maria!" My dad's voice echoes along the empty street, but there's no way I'm looking back.

Whatever I do, I can never go back.

MARIA & MYSTERY GUEST

MARIA:

> Why did you drag my mom and dad into this?!

MYSTERY GUEST:

> You only have yourself to blame.

The sun is fully up now, and I'm standing on the edge of town.

My hands tremble as I type my next message.

MARIA:

> What do you want from me?

MYSTERY GUEST:

> To play a game, yeah? Still bored?

What's that supposed to mean? A puzzle? Are they trying to remind me that they have power over me?

But they lost that power when they gave my mom and dad the poster.

Now they have nothing left to get me with . . .

Until I see the next message.

168

It's not true. It *can't* be true.

But as I get closer to the old warehouse, it's in the air. The smell of burning . . .

"Pip!" I throw my bike onto the grass and run the last part of the way through the woods. When I get to the warehouse, I see flames shooting from the cracked windows.

Where is she?

"Pip!"

Is she *really* here? Why isn't she answering? What if MG is just doing this to get me to go inside?

I take a few steps forward, but I don't dare go any farther. The flames are licking at the walls. The fire feels so hot that it's like I'm burning, even at this distance.

But then a scream comes from inside.

"Maria!"

The scream floods through my body like ice-cold water.

"Pip!"

It's like that night all over again. The night when the church was completely ablaze within a few minutes.

I take a deep breath and jump over the first of the flames. Luckily I'm not wearing anything synthetic, and I make it through without catching fire myself.

"Pip, where are you?"

"Maria!" Again, she screams my name, but that's all she says.

A beam crashes from the ceiling to the floor, exploding into thousands of pieces. The sparks fly in all directions, one of them landing on my bare arm.

"Ow!" I slap the pain away. "Pip, where are you?!"

Pip doesn't answer. My only option is to head deeper into the building.

What if another beam falls and hits me on the head?

I should call the firefighters. They can save Pip.

But what if they don't get here in time?

Jax as a victim was bad enough, but what if Pip doesn't make it?

And all because I insisted on playing a game?

With my arms in front of my face, I take a few more steps forward.

"Mariaaaaaa . . ." Pip's voice sounds distorted, as if her throat is being squeezed.

For a moment, I picture Norah nearly strangling me.

But she'd never do that to Pip.

"Pip!" I feel panic blazing inside my chest. "Pip, where—"

Part of the ceiling comes crashing down, triggering some kind of fireball.

I try to protect my face with my arms, feel my skin burning.

"Pip, I . . ." The pain around my stomach is unbearable. When I look down, I see that my shirt has caught fire.

Frantically I start slapping at it—and then I hear Pip's voice again.

"Mar . . . iaaaaaaaa . . ."

Why does she sound so weird?

But then I see where the voice is coming from.

On the floor, surrounded by debris, is a tape recorder, almost melted by the heat.

PIP

Did Maria know she was going to die?

I don't think so . . .

CODY

Those last moments, she was *so* scared.

Honestly?

It was such an amazing thing to see.

NORAH

Are we finally getting to my favorite part?

MARIA & MYSTERY GUEST

I roll over and over on the sandy ground to make sure the fire is out.

It's a few minutes before I finally dare to stand up.

My shirt is sticking to my stomach, and when I gently pull at it, a strip of skin comes away with it.

I scream.

Pip wasn't there. This was all one big trap, and I walked straight into it.

MG must have known I'd go into the building. They know Pip may be the only person I *really* care about.

My phone feels so hot when I take it out of my pocket.

I drop down onto the ground, and by the edge of the lake, I type my message.

MARIA:

YOU ARE SICK AND DISTURBED!

I'm doubled over with the pain from my stomach. I need to cool the wound right now, so I leave my phone on the sand and crawl over to the lake.

I don't know if wetting my skin is a good plan. I suddenly can't remember anything from the first aid course I did at school.

But anything has to be better than this pain, right?

The last crawl to the lake feels endless.

But then I'm finally there.

First my hands, then my arms, my upper body . . .

It's as if I can hear the water hissing when I finally lay my stomach in it.

I shriek. The pain that was so sharp and burning now becomes stabbing, unbearable.

Back on the shore, my phone makes a sound again.

Is MG ever going to leave me alone?

When I finally return to my phone, their words are dancing before my eyes.

I know this is another trap and that there's no way I should respond.

But the mysterious eye behind the mask seems to wink at me.

And they promised at the start that they'd reveal themself after the fifth game.

With the last of my strength, I type my answer.

MARIA:

Bring it on!

MYSTERY GUEST:

Then you'll have to accept the fifth game.

MARIA:

And that is?

MYSTERY GUEST:

To survive our encounter.

Before I can answer, I hear something over by the warehouse.

Someone is walking toward me, dressed completely in black. They're wearing the mask that I've only seen on-screen until now.

Standing before me is Mystery Guest.

"What . . ." I begin, but they're coming straight at me.

I have no time to react. Their hands are on my throat, and they're pushing me backward.

Their grip is so strong that I can barely defend myself. I hit out, punching and struggling, but it's no use.

They want to kill me.

Is this what they'd been planning all along?

I manage to raise my knee and slam it into their ribs as hard as I can.

There's a groan, and for a moment, I break free.

But then they pounce on me again and drag me toward the water.

They're going to drown me.

The thousands of fireflies will be the last thing I see.

Survive our encounter.

I have to fight. I have to stay alive.

As I go underwater, I feel the stabbing pain in my stomach again.

I can't tell anymore which arm is mine and which is theirs, but I sink my teeth into the flesh.

Again, they let go of me, and I surface, spluttering.

A brief moment of silence. We face each other like gladiators, gasping and exhausted, up to our waists in the water.

"So you want to know who I am?"

I recognize the voice, but it's as if my body can't comprehend it.

"If I let you know who I am, I'll have to kill you, Maria."

"Then so be it," I say, brushing a strand of wet hair out of my face.

Bring it on. I'll finish them.

Up until now I've played all their games. Even on the highway, they didn't defeat me.

If anyone here is going to die, it's them.

"Okay." Mystery Guest grabs the edge of their mask and pulls it from their face.

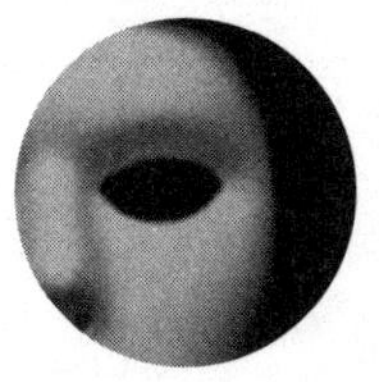

THE FIRE AND THE COURT CASE

PIP & MARIA

"You're drunk."

I look at Maria, but as always, I avoid her gaze.

There's something in her eyes that I can't handle.

"Am not."

"Are so!" Maria chuckles.

Around us the music continues, the thumping bass making me nauseous. Outcast has always been a place I prefer to avoid, but Maria invited me. And you don't say no to Maria—everyone knows that.

It's something about her eyes.

All the teachers are putty in her hands, and all the boys think she's hot.

And some of the girls too.

I'm one of them.

But I always thought she was completely beyond my reach—until she suddenly sat down at my table in the cafeteria.

"You coming tonight?" she asked, and of course I said yes.

"You're cute when you're drunk." Maria holds out her hand and strokes my cheek.

Why is she doing this?

"Maria . . ." I say quietly.

"You're different now," Maria continues.

"Better?"

Maria doesn't reply. She's looking at a group of boys who are a few years ahead of us at school. They're completely out of it. Even now, when I'm a bit drunk, I can tell.

"Who are they?"

"That asshole over there? He's my brother."

"Your brother?" Only now do I see the resemblance. They have the same sharp nose, intensely blue eyes, and brown hair.

"He abuses me," Maria says so suddenly that I gasp.

"What? How?"

"He hits me when he's angry." Maria sighs. "And he's angry a lot of the time."

"I'm sorry. That's really tough," I manage to say.

"No one knows about it," says Maria. "Only you."

Then she gives me a very serious look. "Promise me you won't tell anyone."

"This is my place."

Maria insisted on bringing me home. Now we're standing outside my green front door. I can hardly read our name on the sign. The letters dance before my eyes.

I seriously can't handle alcohol.

I put the key in the lock, and I'm about to head inside when Maria pulls me back.

"Wait."

For a moment, we look at each other, and I feel the same pain as always. Looking at Maria is like being electrified, but not in a good way. Her gaze is . . . too intense.

Then Maria leans forward.

"What are you . . ." I begin, but the rest of my sentence is smothered by her lips.

Maria.

And.

I.

Are.

Kissing.

Maria pulls me against her so tightly that I can hardly breathe. She doesn't let go of me for a few seconds.

"We belong together, Pip," she says. "Don't you agree?"

All I can do is nod. Because if there's anyone I want to belong to, it's her.

I watch Maria go as she walks down the street.

What if this was all some kind of whim? If Maria only likes me when I'm drunk, and this was just a one-off?

But what about what she said? That we belong together?

Maria was drunk too. Maybe tomorrow morning she won't remember anything about it.

Then I see Maria turning right at the end of my street. That's not the right way. She should go left to get to her place!

Is she so drunk that she's forgotten the way?

I'm about to call out to her, but I change my mind and decide to go after her instead.

Walking gradually sobers me up, the alcohol dissolving into the fresh air.

Where is Maria going?

I know I shouldn't be doing this, but my legs are carrying me along. I'm following her like some kind of stalker.

We're at the edge of town now. There's nothing here but an old church.

Is that where she's going? But what does she want *there*, in the middle of the night?

Then Maria stops and looks back over her shoulder. I hide behind a tree just in time, my heart thumping painfully against my ribs.

Did she see me?

But then I hear rustling.

When I look again, I see that Maria has a blue jerry can in her hands.

What on earth is she doing with that?

Without stopping to think about it, I grab my phone and take a photo of her.

Just the one. It's not even in focus.

Then I watch as Maria sprinkles the contents of the jerry can around the church. She throws the last drops onto the white walls.

And then she strikes a match. In the flame, I see her face for a moment, half covered by shadows.

A shiver runs down my spine, but I go on watching.

184

And then Maria throws the match onto the ground.

Wide-eyed, I watch the scene in front of me.

Why did Maria do that?

Because she wants to act tough? But there's no one here to see it!

I remember an article I read recently about pyromaniacs, people who are obsessed with fire.

Is that what's going on with Maria?

She stands silently, watching the sea of flames as the wall starts to crumble away.

The heat reaches all the way to my hiding place among the trees.

What if the woods go up in flames? The fire is already licking greedily at the bushes around the church.

Maria doesn't hesitate for a second; she just runs off.

What should I do? Call emergency services? But then Maria will know I was here.

I watch as the first of the bushes catches fire. If this continues, the fire will soon reach the nearby farms.

Where people are sleeping . . .

Anonymous.

I have to call anonymously.

"Emergency services. How can I help you?"

"Fire! There's a fire!" I shriek. I explain where it is. "Come quickly!"

And then I hang up.

FERRIS & MARIA

"We'd like to ask your son some questions."

I hear strange voices coming from the hall downstairs, but I just turn over in my bed.

To be honest, I don't realize that I'm the son they're talking about.

My head is thumping. It feels like someone's locked up in there, pounding on the inside of my skull to be let out.

"Ferris!" My dad's voice sounds like an order.

"Leave me alone," I groan, but then my bedroom door opens.

"Ferris." This time it's my mom. "Wake up."

Since when did she start just coming into my room like that? My rule is that she always has to knock three times, so that I can say no.

"Hey." I angrily throw off the duvet.

"You need to come downstairs" is all my mom says. "Now."

I don't get it. What's going on? Why won't they just let me sleep it off?

Downstairs I see my dad first, with a black eye.

How did he get that?

But then I see the cops at our front door.

"What the . . ."

"Sweetheart." Mom puts one hand on my shoulder. "Don't say anything. We'll arrange a lawyer for you."

"So you don't remember anything?" The female officer sneers at me.

I know what she's thinking. That I'm faking it.

But that new stuff that Mike got is hella strong.

"That's right."

"Who did you get the drugs from?"

"I don't know." That *is* a lie, but I'm not going to rat on him. Then he'll never sell me anything again.

And the world on drugs is a much better place—feels like I've got more room to breathe.

"So you don't know if you went to the church or not?"

Why do they keep going on and on about that church?

"Will you tell my client why he's here?" my lawyer insists. He's a douchebag in a pin-striped suit. Looks like he stepped straight out of a movie, with his leather briefcase full of documents.

"A fire was started there," the cop says. "And someone saw you at the scene."

"Me? Who said that?"

"We can't tell you that."

"Well, they're lying." I slump in the chair and glare at the police officer defiantly. "You've got nothing on me."

"They sent him to a special center." Maria is lying in my arms on my bed.

When she lies like this with me, it's like I'm holding the whole world. I could lie here for hours, days, months.

Her curls are tickling my face, but there's no way I'm going to move.

"What kind of center?"

"It's this expensive private clinic." Maria sighs. "He has a room of his own with a TV, but, hey. He's gone. That's the important thing. I was so scared that it wouldn't happen, but when he lost it in the courtroom, it was all over. I'm so relieved."

"Yeah." I think back to that night when I saw her with the jerry can. I never told her about it.

And the photo on my phone has been pushed down the screen by dozens of selfies of the two of us.

So we have a shared secret now, even though Maria doesn't know it.

And I'll do whatever it takes to keep that secret.

For her.

For us.

LAST JANUARY

SHANNON'S MURDER

PIP & MARIA

"Want to go do something?" Maria is lying beside me, in my arms, as always.

"We could watch a movie?"

"I meant something different."

I kiss her hair. "This?"

"Something more exciting."

It feels like a punch to the gut.

At that moment, both our phones buzz. Mine is on my desk, but Maria's is in her pocket, and she fishes it out.

"Holy shit," I hear her say. She's looking at our class's group chat.

"What is it?"

"It's Shannon . . ."

"Shannon? Isn't that the girl from . . ."

"She didn't get home from Outcast last night." Maria looks at me, her eyes wide. There's a mixture of surprise and excitement on her face. "She's missing."

PIP & SHANNON

That night I dream about Shannon, even though I barely know her.

I want to join the search team, but they tell me I'm too young.

Too young to find a corpse.

Because it's pretty likely that she's dead . . .

It's all the whole town is talking about, including me and Maria.

We scour the internet, looking for clues.

But after last night at Outcast, no one has seen her alive. She set off for home on her own . . .

And then she was found a few hours later.

Raped.

Murdered.

Strangled in a field.

Maria and I have seen each other every day since then. We stand guard outside Shannon's house. We speculate about her final hours and minutes.

It turns out that Shannon is our "something more exciting."

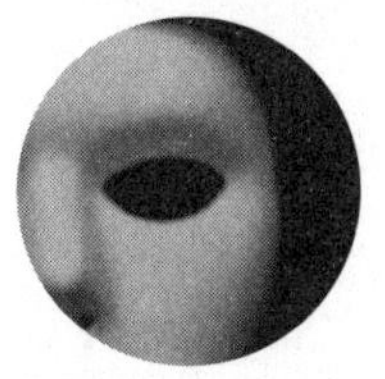

LAST FEBRUARY

THE NIGHT WITH MARIA

MIKE & MARIA

I'm not easily impressed by girls, but Maria is different.

The way she moves, the way she dances—as if she doesn't give a crap about anyone or anything.

Most girls are insecure, but she doesn't seem to know the meaning of the word.

When I'm at the pizzeria with my dad, she comes in to pick up three pizzas.

I follow her with my eyes. It's impossible *not* to watch her.

"Mike," I hear my old man say. "Don't do that."

"What?" I feel like he caught me checking her out.

"You can come home with any girl you like. But not that one."

"Why not?"

"She turned in her own brother."

I know the story about Ferris. Such a hyper guy. I sold him drugs that night, like I did every Friday.

Seems he couldn't handle them that time, so he set the church on fire.

"Big deal. Ferris did it, didn't he?"

"They say she didn't shed a single tear in the courtroom," my dad says. "I just don't trust her."

PIP & MARIA

"Let's go to Outcast on Friday," says Maria.

I shake my head. "We could just watch a movie, couldn't we?"

"Again?" Maria makes a face.

It's another punch to my gut. Why isn't being together enough for her?

"Or we could retrace Shannon's movements again?" I show her the sketches on my desk. "People are saying online that she was lying like this."

"You drew her?" Maria's eyes widen.

"I just did a few sketches," I say defensively. "But there are some new theories about her killer, and . . ."

"It's never going to be solved anyway," says Maria, dismissing the subject. "I want to get drunk tonight. Or more."

"Drugs?" I think about Mike, that creepy guy with the bleached hair. If there's one person I don't trust, it's him.

"If you don't go, I'm going alone," says Maria.

"So you'd rather be there than with me?"

Maria sighs. "Stop being so difficult . . ."

"Difficult?" I can feel panic bubbling up inside me. Why would she say that kind of thing?

"Yes, you're being difficult." Maria is stroking Jax, who's bumping his head against her legs. My cat seems to be as crazy about Maria as I am.

"I just want to get stoned out of my mind," says Maria. "Why are you so boring?"

Boring.

The word slowly trickles into my body, like it's coming from an IV drip.

It reaches my heart, which starts pounding faster and faster.

It seeps into my head, which heats up.

And it takes over my tongue, which flops in my mouth, heavy and dead.

"You might be boring, but you're *my* boring little baby." Maria plants a kiss on my lips. "See you tomorrow."

Maria is alone. Until now that little girlfriend of hers would always come along. I've often seen them here, kissing and that, but this time she's on her own at the bar.

Strangely she doesn't look lonely. She's just standing there, casually watching the dancing crowd.

"Hey." I go and stand beside her. "I'm—"

"Mike," she says. "I know who you are."

"You know my name," I say. "That doesn't mean you know who I am."

"You're the local drug dealer," says Maria. "I've been warned about you."

"Funny, I've been warned about you too, Maria."

Maria's expression changes. She looks at me as if she's *really* seeing me for the first time.

Then she holds out her hand, and I shake it.

"So, Mike . . ." She savors my name on her tongue. "Are you going to buy me a drink or not?"

I forget the drugs for the night. Every now and then, someone comes and asks, but I brush them off.

"You're missing out on a load of income," says Maria after I send the third customer away.

"Ah, it's not a problem," I say dismissively. "It's not like I'll notice."

Maria looks over at my convertible. "Yeah, I guess . . ."

"Want to take a ride?" I run my eyes over her outfit. She's wearing a low-cut top and a pair of shorts.

"Hey, can we?"

"For you? Always." I can hear how cheesy I sound, but Maria doesn't seem to mind. As she walks ahead of me to the car, I watch her curls dancing on her back.

She stops to speak to a group of girls. I think they're in her class at school.

I go sit in the car and hit the horn twice to say that her taxi is about to leave.

Maria opens the door and drops into the passenger seat.

I wave at the girls, who are watching us.

Then we leave Outcast behind.

"Wasn't your girlfriend there tonight?" I ask as we take a stretch of highway.

"She didn't want to come."

Maria's sigh does not escape me.

"What's wrong? Trouble in paradise?"

Maria looks at me. "Of course not."

"I don't understand what you see in that Tip."

"Pip." Maria laughs.

"Whatever, that dead girl. That's who I mean." I step on the gas. "They should have called her RIP: Rest in peace."

Maria's laughter echoes across the quiet highway. Then she suddenly becomes serious.

"Why have people warned you about me?"

"Because you got your own brother locked up. It's true, isn't it?"

There's a moment of silence. But then Maria says, "That's right. Is that a problem?"

"I don't know what your brother did" is all I say.

"He started a huge fire."

"Yeah. But what else?"

"Isn't that enough?" Maria gives me a sidelong look, and I glance back. She has the bluest eyes I've ever seen. I grip the steering wheel a little more tightly. She is so hot.

"Do you hate him?" I ask. "Your brother?"

"Absolutely," says Maria.

"Why?"

"That's none of your business, Mike."

I take the exit toward the fields and race faster than ever before.

"Where are we actually going?" Maria says, looking around. "I don't know this area at all."

"We're looking for a quiet place," I say, shifting a little in my seat. I can hardly take it anymore.

At the first stopping place, I park my convertible. It's a little way off the road, the perfect spot.

"Well, this is exciting," says Maria as I pull the hand brake.

"You like it?" I lean my hand on her headrest, and we look at each other for a long time.

"It feels so good, the way you're just looking at me," says Maria. "Pip can't do that."

"She doesn't know what she's missing. You're so hot, Maria. Did you know that?"

Maria nods with all the certainty in the world. "Yep, I know."

I don't hesitate for another second. I just kiss her.

I don't know why, but I thought she'd play harder to get.

It's kind of disappointing. I enjoy the hunt.

But Maria kisses me back, expertly circling her tongue around mine.

After a few minutes, I stop and look at her.

"How about we move to the back seat?"

She better not say no.

"Hang on just a second." Maria pulls her water bottle from her bag and takes a sip. Then she screws the cap back on and looks at me.

"I'm ready."

In the back seat, I unbutton my pants.

"Hey, do you know how old I am?" Maria asks.

I say an age, but she shakes her head.

"Two years younger."

I'm shocked for a moment, and Dad's voice echoes inside my head. *You can come home with any girl you like. But not that one.*

What will he say if he finds out I'm . . . with a minor?

"Come on," Maria says then. Her eyes look a bit unfocused as she pulls her top down. "It's okay."

My excitement returns in an instant, and I push away my dad's warnings.

When we're getting down to it, I notice her shoving against my chest.

"What's wrong?" I ask her. "Don't you want to?"

"No, that's not it," she says, but then she gives me another shove. She even scratches my face really hard. I feel my cheek tear open.

"What the fuck are you doing?" I look at her. Is she playing some kind of game?

Maria smiles. "Another few seconds and I'm going to pass out."

"Huh? What? What's going on?"

Maria looks at me with a smile. She suddenly seems much older than her age.

"You gave me GHB," she says.

"What?" The rape drug? "What are you talking about?"

"No one's going to believe you, Mike . . ." Maria's voice is suddenly coming from a long way off. Her eyes roll back in her head.

I quickly jump off her and pull up my underwear.

"Maria!" I slap her cheek, but it's no good. Even when I grab Maria's shoulders and shake her frantically, nothing happens.

She is completely unconscious.

I just don't trust her.

My dad's voice has come back.

I look at Maria's bottle, which is still in the passenger seat. What is actually in there?

You gave me GHB. No one's going to believe you.

Slowly the pieces of the puzzle start to fall into place inside my head, and I feel the blood rushing to my face.

"Damn . . ." I whisper. "Damn, damn, damn."

The morning after Maria went to Outcast by herself, she shows up at my door really early.

I see her coming from the kitchen window, wandering down the street. She looks like she can barely stand up straight.

Did she get so drunk at Outcast that she can't walk?

I run to the front door and pull it open.

"What . . ." I begin, but Maria bursts into tears, and I put my arms around her.

She's shaking like crazy. She's even gagging.

I take her to the kitchen and pour a glass of water for her. Hands trembling, she lifts it to her mouth.

"Why . . ." Maria's voice sounds thick with tears. "Why weren't you there last night?"

"I . . ."

"Why did you let me go to Outcast on my own?"

"Because . . ." I shake my head. "What happened?"

"I'm so tired . . ." Maria takes another gulp of water,

but it's like the glass is as heavy as lead. Her hands are still shaking.

"Maria!" I insist.

She drops the glass onto the counter, water splashing in every direction.

"I . . . I think I was raped."

MIKE & HIS DAD

"Pa . . ." My whole body is trembling when I get out of the car. I should never have left Maria by the side of the road, but what was I supposed to do?

Take her home? What could I have said?

Um, hello, Maria's parents, here's your daughter? She took GHB, and we had sex?

If I'm lucky, Maria won't remember a thing when she wakes up. I read somewhere that GHB affects the brain.

Maybe she took just the right amount? I have no idea how much there was in her bottle.

"Mike?" My dad comes out of the shed with a worried look on his face. "You look awful! What the hell happened?"

I feel tears welling up.

"Pa . . ." I collapse into his arms. "Something bad happened . . ."

"We're here to talk to Mike Swan, your son." Two police officers are at our front door. I hear their voices from the kitchen.

My dad made me a mug of coffee, but I haven't drunk any yet.

All I can see is Maria's face. And her limp body by the roadside.

And that bottle of water, which apparently had GHB in it.

This is such unbelievable garbage . . . Maria set me up.

She wants to make me pay for something I didn't even do.

Then I gasp.

The bottle!

That thing is still in the passenger seat of my car!

I was so busy dumping Maria that I completely forgot about it.

What if they impound my car and find the bottle?

No one's going to believe you.

"Mike hasn't done anything," I hear my dad say. "This is a serious misunderstanding, gentlemen. Believe me, my son . . ."

"We'd like to have a word with your son by ourselves, sir."

MIKE & THE TOWN

"There he is." The voices follow me wherever I go. They're a much worse punishment than the community service and compulsory therapy that begin this week.

Maria was right: No one will believe me. Some days I feel like even my dad doubts my story.

"It's just terrible. That scum should be behind bars." The woman in line behind me at the baker's speaks just loud enough for me to hear.

"Yeah, right? If it were my daughter, he wouldn't be walking around here anymore. I'd have made sure of that."

"That poor girl. Putting GHB in her drink. Who would do something like that?"

I turn to look at them. The two older women fall silent.

"She's lying," I say. "Maria screwed me over."

"I thought you were the one who screwed *her*, pal." A guy at the back of the line takes a step forward. "Or am I wrong?"

"She wanted me to."

"She wanted you to drug her? Is that why she scratched your whole face?" He raises his fist. "If it were my sister, I'd beat you to a pulp. And now: Beat it."

PIP & MARIA

"I heard Mike is moving away," I say cautiously to Maria.

Mike is like a hand grenade. You have to be very careful if you drop his name when Maria is around.

"That's good." Maria is stroking Jax nonstop. We're lying on my bed, Jax with his head on Maria's lap and the rest of his body on mine. He feels like *our* cat.

"I'm so sorry," I say quietly. "For not being there that night."

"It doesn't matter." The tone of Maria's voice says the opposite. She must have said, like, ten times that she's so happy that group of girls from school saw her leave with Mike. She'd already told them she didn't entirely trust him but that she wouldn't turn down a ride in his convertible.

I don't understand why she'd get into that creep's car, but I don't dare to say so.

She couldn't have known that he'd put GHB in her water bottle—and certainly not what he'd do after that.

The thought of Maria trying to stop him but that he just kept on going . . .

"You didn't feel like it," Maria says. "That can happen, can't it? You had no way of knowing I'd be raped."

Raped.

Just the word sounds so awful.

I want to say something, but I don't know what. Maria is still stroking Jax. I feel so nauseous.

From that moment on, I decide that I will do anything for Maria.

Anything at all.

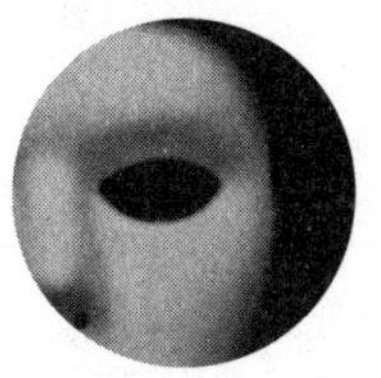

LAST MARCH

NORAH ENTERS THE SCENE

PIP & MARIA

"Everything is just the same . . ." Maria falls back onto her towel with a sigh. It's way too cold by the lake, but she insisted on coming here. For some reason, we never hang out at her place.

Is she ashamed of me?

"What's the same?" I ask.

Maria looks at me and shakes her head. "Never mind."

I know what this conversation is about. The bad feeling spreads through my body again.

But this time I'm going to solve it. I've already figured out how.

"Norah got in touch," I say.

"Norah?" Maria looks at me. "Who's that?"

"My ex."

"You have an *ex*?" Maria stares at me in amazement. It hurts. Like she can't imagine there's someone else out there who might like me.

"Yeah." I decide to crank it up a notch. "My dad really liked her, but we just weren't right for each other."

"Your dad *liked* her?" Maria sits up. "What?"

"Norah was . . . amazing."

"And what did she want?" She sounds suspicious. I've never heard her like that before, and I like it.

"She wants me back," I say.

Maria's eyes narrow.

"No way," she says. "You belong with me."

That's when I know for sure that Norah is the best idea I've ever had.

NORAH & MARIA

What if she recognizes me?

What if she recognizes her own girlfriend behind the curly wig and the red lipstick?

Maybe I should have put on more foundation. I think my stupid freckles are still showing.

Then I see Maria, sitting all alone on the bench opposite Shannon's house.

Which makes sense, because I canceled our date.

I take a deep breath and head straight for her.

"You must be Maria," I say in the voice I've spent so long practicing.

Maria looks up and seems startled. "Norah?"

I described her in detail. Maria wanted to know why I liked her.

I told her she was so cute. She looked like she'd just stepped out of a 1950s commercial.

And I said she was a really good kisser.

Maria became more jealous with every word.

And me? I grew bigger.

"Yes. I'm Norah." I sit down beside her on the bench. "You and I need to talk."

PIP & MARIA

"**I** met your ex." Maria comes up to me at break time.

"Oh." I feel my cheeks burning. "And?"

"She's pretty intense," says Maria, sitting down opposite me at the table. "I don't get what you were doing together. Actually, I don't think I know you as well as I thought, Pip Shipman."

Then she looks straight at me, and I look back at her for a second or two.

"I think you have many faces. And do you know something . . . ?" Maria rests her hand on mine. For the first time, she's looking at me as if she likes me as much as I like her. "I like it."

THE CONVERSATION

PIP & MARIA

"We're going to talk about this just one time," says Maria when we're together at the lake, "and then never again."

I nod, but I have no idea what she wants to talk about.

"Okay." Maria sits cross-legged. "Here's what I suggest: When you're Norah, you should *really* be Norah."

Maria says it so casually that it takes a second to get through to me. But then it feels like I'm tumbling into an abyss.

She knows.

She actually knows!

All those times I showed up as Norah, Maria played along, so I seriously thought I was getting away with it.

But, no. She must have known for ages that Norah and I are one and the same person.

"When you come to me as Norah, I'll treat you like Norah, and you'll treat me as the enemy. Okay?"

I nod, but my heart is still pounding like crazy.

Why isn't Maria mad at me? I pretended to be someone else, and she seems to think it's perfectly normal!

"We won't talk about one with the other. So whatever happens between Norah and me stays between Norah and me. You can't talk about it as Pip, because officially you have no way of knowing. Because you weren't there."

This conversation is insane, but Maria's eyes are sparkling like never before.

"Okay," I hear myself reply.

Maria gives a satisfied nod. "And feel free to make things harder for me."

"What do you mean?"

"Well, you could challenge me a bit . . ." Maria runs her finger over my cheek, and as always, my whole body reacts.

"Just make me terrified of Norah. Okay?"

Is that what she wants? To be terrified?

But you're my *boring little baby.*

First we needed Shannon—and now Norah.

Maybe my so-called ex is the only way Maria will stay with me.

"Okay," I say again.

Maria kisses me. She pushes me back onto my towel, and I feel her weight on top of me.

"I love you, Pip," she whispers in my ear for the first time. "I really do."

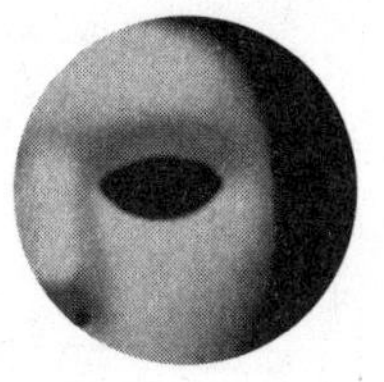

LAST MARCH

THREE PEOPLE MEET

MIKE & FERRIS

"What are you doing here?" says Ferris, nervously glancing around.

The visitors' room is empty, except for one other guy, who's looking our way.

"I've come to visit you," I say. "Isn't that allowed?"

"But why, man? I don't want any drug dealers coming here to see me. Then they'll never let me out early."

"No one here knows I was your dealer," I say. "Listen, I need to talk with you."

"Why?"

"Because we have something important in common."

"And what's that?" Ferris looks at me suspiciously, and I can't blame him after everything that's happened. If your own sister can put you behind bars, anything's possible.

It was only after I left town that I began to see things clearly—and I could only come to one conclusion.

"Maria," I say. "I think she screwed us *both* over."

PIP & MIKE

UNKNOWN NUMBER:

Pip, we need to talk about Maria.
Will you call me?

PIP:

Who is this?

UNKNOWN NUMBER:

Mike.

PIP:

WTF? I have nothing to say to you, you disgusting rapist!

UNKNOWN NUMBER:

I didn't do it. I might be a bit shady, but I didn't rape her.

Maria's lying.

Just like she lied about Ferris.

Pip?

You still there?

Ferris didn't start that fire. Believe me.

It was Maria. She's been playing everyone. Probably including you.

Pip?

PIP:

Is typing . . .

PIP & FERRIS

"**I**'m Pip." I hold out my hand to the boy standing opposite me. Although we often saw each other at school, I've never spoken to him before.

"Pip." Ferris looks at me suspiciously and remains standing behind his chair. I guess the last thing he was expecting was a visit from his sister's girlfriend.

"What are you doing here?"

I look around. The visitors' room is very different than I expected. Lighter, cleaner, nicer.

"We need to talk about Maria."

"What? You too?" Ferris says with a frown. "Mike was here this week."

"I know. I came because of him."

I have a stomachache again just thinking about it. The thought of secretly being in touch with Maria's rapist and her brother feels like the ultimate betrayal.

What is she going to do if she finds out about this? She must never find out—*never*.

"I want your word that you won't tell Maria about this," I say. "This meeting never happened."

"Okay . . ." Ferris slowly sinks down into his chair. He's still looking at me like he can't believe I'm here.

"I don't think you started the fire."

"You don't *think* I did?" Ferris frowns again.

"No." I pause. "I *know* you didn't. I have proof."

That last word makes Ferris look directly at me. His eyes are even harder to look at than his sister's.

"What have you got?"

I lean forward across the table. "A photo."

"A photo?" Ferris's suspicion seems to be slowly slipping away. "What of? Maria?"

I hesitate again. I swore to myself that I'd keep the photo a secret forever.

But that was *before* I knew about Mike. At first I didn't believe him, but then he started talking about the fire . . . After all, Maria had pinned that on someone else too.

"I need to know I can trust you first," I say.

Ferris slumps back and crosses his arms.

"I could say the same thing to you. Why are you here?"

I pause and think about it.

If Maria lied about the fire and the rape, she could have been lying about other things too.

I even doubt her story about that lookout tower in the woods. She said she'd been up there. She told me she'd stood on the railing for minutes because she'd wanted to commit suicide.

Then, a few weeks later, she said she'd never climbed the tower.

And there was that time she told me a story about a dog whose life she'd saved.

She said she'd found this emaciated golden retriever tied to a tree. So she took him to the animal shelter in the next town.

But when I asked at the shelter the next day, they didn't know anything about a golden retriever.

But I did stay and get a job there, because it's such a great place.

Why did she lie to me?

I think of Maria, with her steel-blue eyes. That look of confidence, which I fell head over heels for.

What if she really did lie about Mike?

What if Mike is right and she took the GHB herself?

Is she really capable of that? That lie is way worse than lying about a dog.

I remember Maria sitting in the kitchen, completely out of her mind. Maria making me feel guilty for not being there that night . . .

What if she did it just so she could push me around?

Did she really think I'd never find out?

"I want to show Maria that people see through her lies," I say.

"That sounds pretty vague," says Ferris.

"If you agree to help, I'll show you the whole plan."

Ferris clearly has his doubts.

"Mike is in on it too."

The thought of working with that guy makes me uneasy, but I have no choice.

I need both of them. They have to stir things up while I focus on Maria.

Maria probably thinks I'm an easy victim, but I'm going to prove her wrong.

"I want to see the photo," says Ferris. "Then I'll help."

He's as obstinate as his sister—he won't take no for an answer either.

I give in. "Okay," I say, taking the printed photograph from my pocket.

Fortunately I was allowed to bring that in here. I had to hand in my phone at the entrance.

When I put it on the table, Ferris leans forward.

"I *knew* it . . ." he hisses, and then he slams the photograph with his hand. "I am going to kill her."

LAST JUNE

THE PLAN

PIP & THE PLAN

MYSTERY GUEST—NOTES

- Buy phone and prepaid card
- Buy mask
- Create profile picture

How can I send messages when Maria is sitting next to me?

Planned messages. one each time.

Five challenges?

But what?

Based on Maria's lies!

- Drink an unknown liquid (Mike and the GHB)
- The lookout tower (suicide)
- Jax on the highway (This one hurts, but do it anyway! Because of the golden retriever lie.)
- The fire (How to get Maria into the building?)
- THE CONFRONTATION (Aim: To show Maria I'm not as easy to manipulate as she thinks.)

Take a knife, make her TERRIFIED! Then she'll never call me boring or safe again. And she'll know she can't just get away with the things she does.

Maria will need some help with the challenges.

Encouragement?

Who from?

Me?

<u>New character?</u>

CODY = an ally

Can I become yet another person?

YES!

DO IT!

He's here on vacation.

Get him to take photos. Maybe he can ask Maria about the lookout tower?

His dad is aggressive, like Ferris. Creates a connection?

Cody is a daredevil. Maria is going to love him.

LAST JULY

THE START OF THE PLAN

MYSTERY GUEST & MARIA

Maria is crying again.

Since I started paying attention, I've noticed that she often does that when she wants something from me.

And even now I hug her as she sits there, crying on my bedroom floor.

She just climbed up the drainpipe.

"It's Ferris . . ."

She tells me that he's staying all summer and that the summer is going to be a disaster.

"We are not going to let that happen," I say. "How about we do something fun tomorrow?"

"What kind of fun? There's nothing fun around here."

She says it seriously, even though I'm sitting there right in front of her.

Then she asks me if I'm still mad about this afternoon.

"A bit." I turn my face away to emphasize my feelings. "You called me 'safe.'"

That word makes my blood boil again. How dare she say that?

"So?" Maria doesn't seem to have noticed anything.

"'Safe' is the same as 'boring.'"

"That's simply not true."

Silence.

"Do I have to tell you how attractive you are? How sexy? How—"

"Maria . . ." Slowly I feel myself softening again, like butter melting in a pan. Why do I still keep falling for this?

"How wildly desirable, how fun, how fabulous, how—"

I kiss her. Anything to shut her up.

When Maria is outside, I grab my extra phone.

This is the perfect moment.

I look at the profile picture I created a few days ago. It's mysterious, unrecognizable, and menacing. In short: It's perfect.

MYSTERY GUEST:

Bored?

I picture Maria standing on my street right now, looking at the message. Is she going to bite?

I have to stop myself from peeking through the window. That would ruin the whole operation.

She might ignore the message or block the number, and that'll be the end of it.

But then my phone buzzes.

MARIA:

> Always.

Always.

Even when she's with me?

Any lingering doubts about my plan disappear.

Hands trembling, I type a message back to her.

MYSTERY GUEST:

> Let's play a game.

AUGUST

MARIA'S MURDER

MARIA & MYSTERY GUEST

Finally.

Finally I'm going to find out who Mystery Guest is.

As the mask comes off their face, it's as if all the fireflies above the lake stand still.

And then . . .

I see Cody.

And I see Norah.

And I see Pip.

I see all three of them.

They were always three separate people, but now they merge into one face.

PipCodyNorah.

My Pip, with her cute blond hair, her green eyes, and more freckles than ever.

Cody, with his mysterious gaze, who dares to look right at me, for seconds at a time.

And Norah, with the most terrifying grin I've ever seen on anyone's face.

It's all three of them.

"What . . ." I begin.

"I'm not as boring as you thought, am I?" says Pip with a smile. "Or are you going to tell me you saw Cody coming?"

"No . . ." I remember the moment when the strange boy spoke to me in the center of town. I recognized Pip right away, but I didn't understand why she suddenly looked so different. Then, when she introduced herself, I realized.

She'd come up with someone else. A new character.

First there was Norah, and now there was Cody too.

"He wants to know what it's like to kill someone," says Pip. "Did you know that?"

Paralyzed, I stare at my girlfriend.

"The two of them keep nagging away at me," Pip continues. *"Go on! Kill her! Do it, do it!"*

Pip reaches her hand into the pocket of her black hoodie and takes out a knife. The sharp blade glints in the sun.

All the fireflies start moving again, flying crisscross through the air.

"Pip . . ."

"Why did you lie, Maria? Why did you tell so many lies?"

"Me?" I keep my eyes fixed on the blade. "What . . . what are you talking about?"

"You're not going to tell me you didn't recognize those challenges, are you? They all had to do with *your* lies." Pip points the knife at me.

The drink . . .

Mike. But how does Pip know about that?

The lookout tower . . .

My suicide story? It wasn't a lie. I *really* wanted to do it at that moment. I just never went up the tower.

Does that make it a lie?

Jax . . .

I remember the golden retriever whose life I supposedly saved. I wanted to impress Pip. It was just a little white lie. And she got a nice part-time job out of it, didn't she?

The fire . . .

She can't know about that either.

Unless . . .

Of course. Pip *is* Mystery Guest. She's the one who was there that night. She must have followed me to the church.

Panic flares up inside my chest.

"Pip," I say. "I had to get rid of Ferris. Don't you understand? He always hurt me. I was so scared of him. I . . ."

"Lies," says Pip. "Always so many lies. And you kept calling me boring. You're only interesting because of the stories you make up. So I did the same."

Norah, Cody, Mystery Guest.

"Okay, working with Mike and your brother was pretty fucked up. Your brother didn't want anything to do with me at first. He thought I was in on the plot. He almost started to think he was guilty. Did you know that?"

Ferris . . .

I remember my brother when he threw the bricks at me. He asked me if I seriously believed he'd started the fire.

I said that maybe he didn't remember exactly what happened that night.

"Ferris had to go, Pip."

"And Mike? Why did *he* have to go?"

"He's a drug dealer."

"So? You can always find drugs around here, with or without him." Pip's eyes narrow. "Did you need Mike just to make me feel guilty?"

"Of course not." My answer comes quickly, *too* quickly.

"You played all of us." Pip sighs. She doesn't sound angry—more like she's tired. As if I'm a little kid who's just scribbled all over the recently painted walls yet again.

"We all let it happen. You even played me and Cody against each other! Why was Cody allowed to meet your family?"

"You could have met them too, but . . ."

"You said you weren't ready to kiss anyone else when you'd just been kissing Cody!"

"You weren't supposed to talk to each other!" I shout. "Those were the rules!"

"*Rules?*" Pip takes a step forward. "*Rules?!* Go to hell with your rules, Maria. I'm the one who came up with Norah and Cody, so I decide who talks to who."

Pip seems to have forgotten that she's carrying a knife. She's waving her arm around. The blade almost hits me.

Startled, she takes a step back and looks at the knife in her hand.

"Pip . . ." I look at her. "Let go of the knife. You're not a killer."

As I say that last word, she looks at me. Pip's eyes focus on mine. I see Cody's gaze, Norah's grin, and Pip's freckle mustache. I can't tell where one stops and the others begin.

We should never have played this game. I want to turn back time to December last year, when we sat together on the beanbags.

The night when Pip was so drunk that I took her home.

Before the fire, before Shannon's murder, before Mike, before Norah, before Cody . . .

I want to make it all undone.

"Pip?"

I take a step forward. I need to grab that knife off her right now.

Pip's eyes flash from the knife in her hand to me and back again.

"Just give me the knife. It's over, okay?"

Pip shakes her head frantically. "Don't move. I'll . . ."

"This isn't you." I take another step forward. I've almost reached her now. "I *know* you. Come here."

I hold out my arms to her. I want to give her a hug, to reassure her. Then she'll realize that she doesn't want to hurt me. She'll realize that she still loves me, just like I still love her.

At first I think she's going to hug me back.

But then it happens.

She shoves me away.

"Don't touch me!"

I feel a sharp pain in my stomach.

We both look down. All I can see is the handle. The whole blade has bored its way inside me.

"Maria . . ." Pip's face is as pale as death. I don't see a trace of Cody or Norah now, only Pip.

The sweetest girl I ever met.

The girl who only lost her mind because of *me*.

It was me who broke her.

"Pip . . ." Her face blurs, and my knees buckle.

"No!" Pip's shriek is like an animal's. "Maria, no!"

PIP

She's not coming back, is she?

"Dead" means "dead."

This wasn't the idea at all.

You have to understand that it was an accident.

I just wanted to scare her.

I'm so sorry.

Oh, I'm so, so sorry!

CODY

Killing someone is the best thrill ever.

It's too bad that the unbeatable feeling always fades away so quickly.

And then you have to chase the thrill again.

NORAH

Maria is finally dead.

Did it really have to take *so* long?

The worst thing is that Pip regrets it.

She doesn't understand that Maria deserved this 100 percent.

But now Pip is in intensive therapy, as if she's the one with a screw loose.

Without Maria she'd never have ended up that way.

As for that Pomme . . .

Who the hell is the girl Pip's writing letters to now?

Pip says that Pomme understands her. She's told that girl everything.

Okay, then, Pomme needs to die.

As soon as possible.

SEPTEMBER

ONE MONTH LATER

MIKE

I can't wait to get out of this town again.

Maria's murder, the funeral. It all brings up too many memories.

I see my dad waving in the rearview mirror. I think he's glad to see me go too.

He doesn't say so. He'll never say so, but he doubts my version of that night with Maria. He still doubts me.

But I didn't do anything.

I didn't touch her!

At least, not without her consent!

At the funeral, we stood some distance away from her family, because no one wanted us there.

But Dad thought we should go.

I give my dad a quick wave and hit the gas. Away from here, as fast as I can.

I drive past the spot where I saw Maria at the end of July. She nearly had a heart attack when I slowed down and spoke to her. She looked like she'd seen a ghost!

And then I drive past the lookout tower. Pip told me and Ferris all about everything that happened. Turns out Maria really did go stand on the edge.

And then I see the highway, where I dropped off Maria and Cody.

Cody?

Pip.

Man, that girl really is disturbed.

She has an incredible brain, but she is so, so disturbed.

And then I see the church, which burned down last year.

How could Maria have been so ice-cold and given evidence against her brother like that?

The girl had no soul. I should have known.

This town is full of psychos.

Yeah, like I said. I'm glad I'm getting out of here.

I hit the gas harder as I drive past the fields.

That's where Shannon was found.

It was a risk to say my dad was on the search team, but I had to put extra pressure on Maria. I wanted to scare her, and I think it worked out pretty well.

In reality, it was never revealed exactly where Shannon was found. My dad wasn't on the search team at all.

But Shannon really was here, behind that fence.

So how do I know she was found in that exact location?

Like I said: This town is full of psychos.

So, can you keep a little secret?

AUTHOR'S NOTE

Three people confess to a murder.

Why would that ever happen? Some time ago, I listened to a podcast about a real-life murder case. It involved a girl who pushed her boyfriend so far that he killed her mother for her. The girl had been abused by her mother for years.

It was a terrible case, but what fascinated me about it were the role-playing games that the girl engaged in with her boyfriend in the period leading up to the murder. They were in touch online, and she pretended to be different people. She had a "romantic" character, for instance, and also a very "dark" one. Their role-playing seems to have been the start of their murder plans, and they egged each other on.

It was the role-playing in that case that stayed with me.

I decided to use it for this story.

Pip makes up Norah first, but later the sinister Cody comes along—and, of course, Mystery Guest. Pip makes up more and more stories to make Maria stay with her. She doesn't realize that she's slowly losing herself in the process.

This book was a tough roller coaster to write. I constantly needed reminders to know who I was writing about. All of the roles merged into one another. And whose side was I on as a writer? I'm not entirely sure.

Because, to be fair: Who is the victim here? And who is the culprit?

GET SCARED WITH MAREN STOFFELS!

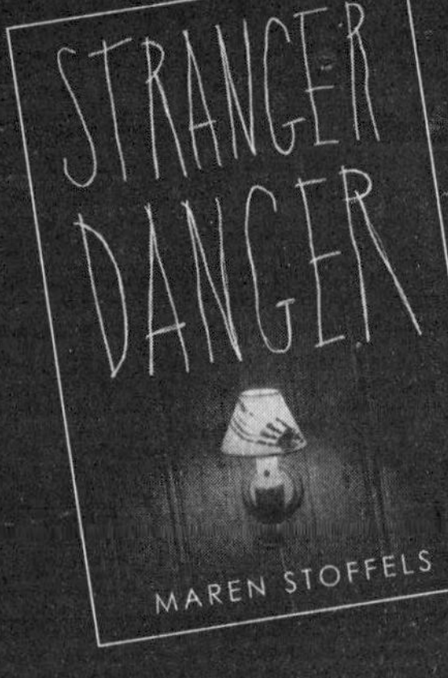